POWER

A LA RUE FAMILY CRIME THRILLER

RICHARD WAKE

SIGN UP FOR MY READING GROUP AND RECEIVE A FREE NOVELLA!

I'd love to have you join my on my writing journey. In addition to receiving my newsletter, which contains news about my upcoming books, you'll also receive a FREE novella. Its title is *Ominous Austria*, and it is a prequel to my first series.

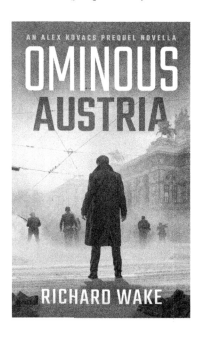

The main character, Alex Kovacs, is an everyman who is presented with an opportunity to make a difference on the eve of the Nazis' takeover of Austria. But what can one man do? It is the question that hangs over the entire series, taking Alex from prewar Austria to the Cold War, from Vienna, to Switzerland, to France, and to Eastern Europe.

To receive *Ominous Austria*, as well as the newsletter, click here:

https://dl.bookfunnel.com/ur7seb8qeg

PART I

SUNDAY AT VINCENT'S

Sunday afternoon, the first Sunday of the month, the back table at Vincent's. For Henri La Rue and the rest of the La Rue family, this was the other holy day of obligation. There was nothing particularly warm or loving about the gathering, and nothing spiritual about it — other than that money was the family religion, and that the first Sunday of the month was Gérard's envelope day.

For years, Sylvie had been threatening to forego the family-style roast pork or roast chicken (on alternating months) and order off of the card, but she never did. This was true mostly because, in the end, she got a lot more pleasure out of the complaining than she would have out of the brisket, or the pig's knuckle, or whatever else was on offer. They had been married long enough that Henri knew this intuitively. It just wouldn't be the first Sunday of the month if Sylvie wasn't bitching about how cheap Uncle Gérard was.

As in, "I mean, what is the old fossil saving it for? It isn't as if he can bury the loot with him when the time comes — and it's coming quick. Christ, look at him."

Gérard sat at the head of the table, his face in shadow, but it was still easy to see that he looked like hell. His oldest friend, Maurice — Silent Moe to everyone, for obvious reasons — sat in his customary spot to Gérard's right, and Father Lemieux — Gérard's priest — sat in what had more recently become his customary spot to Gérard's left. The three of them at the end, the priest carrying the conversation, Silent Moe nodding a lot, Gérard in the middle, Gérard deteriorating a little more every month. His health had been the topic of sub rosa family conversations for a while — and whatever was wrong with him, it wasn't getting any better. Sylvie was incorrect, though. It wasn't coming quick. Gérard's decline had been slow — months long, six, eight, maybe 10 months long. And unless something had changed in recent weeks, Gérard still had not been to see a doctor.

The man was a creature of habit — Mass every morning at Sacré Coeur; toast and marmalade and coffee for breakfast; suit jacket one size bigger than the pants to accommodate the holster he always wore and the pistol he never fired; platters of roast pork or roast chicken at Vincent's. All of that, and no visits to doctors, whom the old man referred to as "well-educated charlatans" when he wasn't calling them "nicely dressed thieves."

The last time he went on his "nicely dressed thieves" rant, Henri nearly spit out his coffee and said, "Pot, kettle?"

"Meaning what?" Gérard said.

"Meaning exactly what you think it means. Come on. Nicely dressed thieves? Have you looked in a mirror lately? Are you that lacking in self-awareness?"

"I'm perfectly self-aware. The difference is, I come by my theft honestly. There is no pretense. I am what I am — and I am not a well-educated charlatan who sometimes pretends to hand you an answer but always wraps his bullshit in an invoice."

"Speaking of bullshit, you know that you've been signed up for SHI since it started. We make the payments every year. Insurance, uncle. No bullshit wrapped in an invoice anymore. Not since the war."

Gérard again yelled about "well-educated charlatans," among other insults.

The memory was interrupted by a coughing fit coming from the end of the table. It sounded as if Gérard was hacking up a lung, and Silent Moe and Father Lemieux were each poised for action, Moe with a glass of water and the priest with a napkin. At one point, Henri's wiseass of a son theatrically wiped at his cheek, as if Gérard had nailed him with some spittle from 15 feet away.

"Christ," said Guy, the son. "He's more dead than alive."

At which point, Guy poked Henri with his elbow and nodded toward the platter of pork. Henri handed it over and the 26-year-old refilled his plate. Sylvie watched and tut-tutted quietly, but her son heard her.

"Better than your cooking," he said. At which point, the mother picked up her knife and menaced it at her oldest. Of course, this — the brandished knife — was something Guy saw on a monthly basis at the two brothels that he ran for the family.

"Take your best shot," Guy said. Then he leaned over, kissed his mother on the cheek, and swiped the roll from her bread plate.

Getting Guy into the business had been good for all of them. Much of the surliness was gone. That he still drank too much and stayed out too late was true, but at least he managed to shave and put on a fresh suit most of the time. And if he and Henri weren't exactly close, father and son were somehow a bit tighter now that "employer and employee" had been added to their relationship résumé.

Then there was Clarice. If Henri had been reluctant to bring Guy into the family business — and he had been, never trusting in the boy's competence — he was adamant that his 23-year-old daughter would not get within a million miles of the La Rue family enterprises. He was proud of her brain and her initiative — she had gone to school for a degree in finance in Zurich, one of only two women in her class, and was finishing up an extra bit of post-graduate coursework at the Sorbonne. She was too smart, too good, with too much potential, and she was not going to be handing anybody an envelope — not as long as Henri had anything to say about it. And that would be for quite a while, seeing as how he was essentially the family's managing partner as it was — and if Gérard continued to decline, he would be more than that.

The fights between father and daughter over this issue had been fierce — and, in this one case, Sylvie tended to side with her husband. She was more old school than Henri in that she didn't think there was a place for women in the business, other than as unofficial counselors to their husbands. Henri was less a traditionalist than Sylvie was that way. He wasn't against a woman taking a seat at the table — just this particular woman, his daughter. The result of the arguments had been, and continued to be, a condition of permafrost in the house, with Clarice often finding an excuse to stay with various friends who had apartments near the Sorbonne.

Still, she had come to the last couple of lunches. And even if she mostly pushed the food around her plate, and whispered conspiratorially to her brother, and pretty much ignored her parents, it was something.

———

I t was in the little back room behind the back table at Vincent's where Henri always took the best measure of his uncle. After dessert, Gérard would get to his feet and go through the door, accompanied by Silent Moe. That was where the real business of the afternoon was conducted, in age order: first Henri, then his brother Martin, then his cousin Michel. Guy and Clarice would follow after that, but theirs were only quick social visits. They didn't carry sealed white envelopes in their breast pockets.

The mystery this day was Michel, his chair empty. His wife, Romy, was there, but not the man himself. She had announced when she arrived that "Michel has been detained on a work matter. He'll be here soon." But the coffee was being poured, and still no Michel. Henri looked at Martin, and they both shrugged, and the older brother began the parade into the back room.

"Sit, sit," Gérard said, pointing at the small arm chair. Silent Moe handed him a small glass of brandy, and Henri took a long sip. Then he reached into his pocket for the envelope. It was all a part of the ritual — sit, sip, serve the master.

And then Gérard held out his hand.

There were three main business arms to the La Rue family enterprises — four, if you counted the street money that everyone was permitted to lend out within specified territories. Even Gérard still had a small street operation — although, as Martin put it, "His guys are as old as he is. Tough to break someone's legs when you have a 70-year-old trying to chase the guy down."

So, three arms. Henri handled the bread and butter — thefts from the train station as well as whorehouses and gambling, especially Trinity One, the combination casino/brothel in the 9th, down near the Opéra, that attracted only the wealthiest clients and was the crown jewel of the operation. Martin handled alcohol in all of its forms, running a legitimate wine and liquor importing business that covered for the real operation: supplying bars and cafés with beer and wine whether they wanted it or not. Then there was Michel, the cousin who grew up in Marseille and brought the heroin smuggling business with him to the La Rue family in Paris. Heroin had become the most lucrative part of the operation and also the most controversial — at least to Henri and Martin, who very much liked the additional income but very much hated that their younger cousin had control over so much cash.

Henri handed the envelope to Gérard, and he weighed it in his hand. If it felt light, he tended to say something. If it felt appropriate or heavy, he tended to nod but say nothing — not a "thank you," not a "good job," nothing.

That day, Gérard weighed it for what seemed like an extra-long time, but he said nothing. Just a nod.

In their envelopes, Henri, Martin and Michel each delivered two percent of their gross revenues for the previous month. That was Gérard's take, and it involved the simplest math — two percent was two percent — but it wasn't all that the old man received for, as Sylvie said, "Sitting on his ass and getting in the way." Because there was another financial reckoning that usually took place on a quarterly basis, the distribution of profits after salaries and expenses. It tended to be about 15 percent of the gross, and that amount was split four ways between Gérard, Henri, Martin and Michel.

Gérard handed the envelope to Silent Moe, then took a sip of his own brandy. His hand shook.

"You feeling okay?" Henri said.

"Fine. Getting old is a bitch, but fine."

"You sure?"

"Stop," Gérard said. "I'm fine."

"But, a doctor—"

"Will you fucking stop — I'm fucking fine."

"Well, you don't—"

"I'm not going to warn you again."

"It's just—"

Gérard glared at him, and Henri stopped.

The envelopes he had brought Gérard were smaller than they had been six months earlier, but the old man was fine with that. A year earlier, the La Rues had taken over control of both the Gare du Nord and the Gare de l'Est from a rival family that was in the midst of a crisis. Six months later, the La Rues were forced to make a deal with another rival, the Levines, to give them the Gare de l'Est in exchange for ending what was very nearly a full-on war.

It was a deal that Gérard had quietly brokered with Old Joe

Levine, although neither Henri nor Levine's son, David —
Henri's counterpart — knew all of the details.

"Better this way," Gérard said. He seemed to know what
Henri was thinking without his nephew saying anything.

"Lighter envelopes are never better, uncle."

"Better than a shooting war."

"I guess," Henri said.

M artin followed Henri into the back room. Michel's chair
was still empty. Henri disliked both of them but for
opposite reasons. The problem with Martin was that Henri
knew him too well. The issue with Michel was that Henri barely
knew him at all.

Martin always spent the least amount of time with Gérard —
five minutes, tops. There was no grand strategy to be discussed
with the youngest La Rue brother, and Gérard had little time for
fools, and Martin was, if not a full-fledged fool, at least fool-ish.
While he was in with their uncle, Sylvie said, "Anything?"

"Like what?"

"Deathbed confession? Revised will and testament? I don't
know."

"He's not dying," Henri said.

Sylvie arched an eyebrow.

"At least, he's not dying tomorrow. I mean, he looks like shit,
but if I had to guess, there are miles to go."

Just then, Father Lemieux crouched between their two
chairs and whispered, "I heard what you were saying."

"And what of it?" Sylvie said. She had no time for the man
she referred to as "the briefcase priest" because of his job
working with the cardinal on the archdiocese's finances. The
way he told it, Lemieux had never been a pastor anywhere, just

9

an assistant. But he lived in the big rectory near Notre Dame and had the cardinal's ear, and that wasn't nothing.

"It's just, I'm also worried," the priest said. "This has been going on for too long, and he won't see a doctor, and..."

His voice trailed off. Henri said, "Can't you convince him?"

"About the doctor? Impossible. Such a smart man, but such an imbecile about the medical profession."

"So, what?" Sylvie said. The tone was beyond disrespectful. Henri felt like grabbing her by the hair and reminding her that, if it hadn't been for a bit of subterfuge engineered by Lemieux a few months earlier, her son might have been imprisoned following a bank robbery. By Henri's reckoning, his wife's gratitude could be measured in mere hours — and no more than days.

"I don't like it and I don't like him," is where Sylvie always ended up. "What the hell is he up to?"

"He's Gérard's friend," Henri said.

"So why did he move in?"

"I don't think it's full-time."

"You know what Guy says."

"Guy has sex and conspiracy on the brain. Gérard's too old for that — even if he was interested, which I don't believe. I mean, there was always the story about that girl who died—"

"A story," Sylvie said.

"He's a friend to an old man, and we're lucky for it," Henri said. "I mean, Moe still has his wife to go home to for dinner, and the nights alone for Gérard must be... Christ, do you want to spend time with him?"

"Like he'd ever invite us over — and don't start with the almighty annual Christmas drink. Some goddamned invitation."

That's how the conversation went every time the subject of Lemieux came up. Sylvie didn't like Gérard and she didn't like anybody who liked Gérard, and that was that. It was her transitive property of relationships, and it was immutable. Lemieux would have had to have been brain dead not to sense the hostility, but he never shied away from a conversation.

"I don't know what to do at this point," Lemieux said. "He won't listen to me. I've gotten Maurice's ear, but he doesn't seem to be making a lot of progress — not that he says very much. Part of me thinks I should just bring a doctor around to the house, but, well, no."

"He deserves his dignity," Henri said.

"Yeah, that's what I keep coming back to, even if he is an imbecile."

Lemieux smiled weakly, stood up, and went back to his seat. Henri looked at his watch. If the past was an accurate predictor, Martin would be out in two minutes.

———

Michel had taken off his jacket and tie, his shirt and his undershirt, his shoes and socks and trousers. He stood there in his boxer shorts, on the dirt floor of a garage that was maybe four blocks from Vincent's restaurant, and swung the tire iron he held in his right hand, swung it in a wide arc that ended precisely in the center of Frankie Brière's left kneecap.

Brière screamed, and not for the first time — but the rag stuffed into his mouth and tied into place managed to muffle most of it. Michel had a system when it came to this kind of thing, starting by flattening the subject's nose and frightening him with all of the blood, and then proceeding as necessary. It was why he stripped after tying up Brière — because he still had plans to attend the family lunch, and there would be no time to go home for a fresh change of clothes.

Based on what he knew about Brière, Michel thought the broken nose might be enough. But Brière surprised him. The broken nose produced only a "fuck you" in reply. Next, Michel pulled down Brière's trousers, put on his right shoe, and kicked Brière in the balls as hard as he could. There was no "fuck you" that time, only a first and then a second spew of vomit.

When Brière's breathing approximated normal again, Michel asked him for the fourth time — all four times without raising his voice — "Frankie, I need the delivery details."

Then came another "fuck you." Then came the gag, and then the tire iron that shattered the knee cap. That did the trick — that and a gentle massage of Brière's right knee cap with the tire iron. The details — a vegetable truck with the stencil of a tomato painted on the side, at Les Halles, on Thursday morning at 2 a.m. — were accompanied by tears, and that was the only disappointment Michel felt. Because he admired Frankie's toughness and bravery, and the tears diminished them. It was what he was thinking about, that disappointment, as he finished Frankie's final Sunday afternoon with one, two, three blows to the head with the tire iron.

One, two, three. Michel washed his hands in a nasty sink, and got dressed, and walked the four blocks to Vincent's restaurant. His wife greeted him with a hug, and Henri with mock applause. It wasn't a minute after he walked in that Martin emerged from the back room, signaling that it was Michel's turn.

Henri: "So, what do you think about him?"

Martin: "Looks like shit, same as always."

Henri: "Not Gérard. What do you think about Michel?"

Martin: "The fucking golden child? Same as ever, I guess."

Henri: "But, he missed..."

Martin: "He missed the crap food but he made it for the main event. I'm sure, whatever his excuse, uncle will weigh the slight with one hand and the envelope with the other hand, and..."

Henri: "I guess."

Martin: "You don't guess. You know. You've known for as long as you've had hair on your balls. Hell, you coined the phrase."

Henri: "In the La Rue family, it doesn't matter what's in your head or what's in your heart as long as there's something in the envelope."

Martin: "Here he comes. That was quick."

Henri: "Smug little prick."

Martin: "In his case, he could wipe his ass with the envelope and Gérard would still accept it happily."

Henri: "Smug little prick."

———

Michel came out and Guy took his place in the back room. There was no envelope involved. Guy kicked up only to his father — 10 percent of the gross revenues from the two brothels. He kept another 10 percent for his own salary. After paying all of his expenses — from the girls, to the bartenders, to the security men, and the rest — Guy had to find a way to kick 15 percent into the big pot that Gérard, Henri, Martin and Michel split on a quarterly basis. It was almost never a problem. And in the months when there was more than about 18 percent left after expenses, the rest went into Guy's pocket by means of some creative accounting. Plumbing emergency one month, electrician another, and on and on.

This wasn't a business meeting, then, even if everything about the La Rue family was business.

"You look like hell," Gérard said.

"That's supposed to be my line."

"Meaning?"

"You own a mirror?"

"I'm fine," the old man said. "But you, every time I see you, you're hung over. Or worse."

"I work nights in a whorehouse — how do you expect me to look?"

"It's not the work that exhausts you, it's the play."

Guy saluted. His uncle smiled.

"Any complaints with my performance?"

"That's your father's department, and if he has any, he hasn't expressed them to me. But, you know, I worry."

"No need."

"I can't help it. I just worry—"

"That I'm not cut out for the family business?" Guy said. "Aren't we done with that?"

Gérard took a sip from his drink. Guy had already downed his and held up the glass for Moe to refill.

"I don't know," Gérard said. "It's just, for the longest time..."

"With all due respect, that's bullshit. For the longest time, I was a kid. Granted. Guilty. But my father was a kid once, and you were a kid once — you know, before we had electricity or toilet paper..."

"I could wipe my ass with your face if you're not careful," Gérard said, and then he laughed.

"And you know my father is watching," Guy said. "And you know he can feel how heavy his envelope from me is, and you know that all of you pay pretty close attention to what I throw into the pot every month because I'm my father's son. And there's nothing to bitch about. And the reason there's nothing to bitch about is that I'm pretty fucking good at this, as it turns out."

"You sound surprised."

"I am, a little — but don't you ever tell my father I said that."

The two brothels he ran catered to different clientele. The

one, farther up the butte in Montmartre, was a bit higher class — not like Trinity One, but not bad. The other whorehouse, on Boulevard de Clichy, was universally known in the family as "the skank place." But Guy had made the decision, despite some skepticism from above, to spend some not-insignificant money to class-up the skank place, at least a bit — and it was beginning to pay off.

"I still don't know, putting money in that, in that shithole," Gérard said.

"That's the whole point," Guy said. "Working men have a right to clean, disease-free dicks, too — and to a relaxing complimentary drink after they've put their clean, disease-free dicks away."

Gérard laughed and waved at Silent Moe. He poured them each another half-shot of the brandy.

"We're both working men, right?" the old man said, raising his glass. "In that case, I drink to clean, disease-free dicks."

———

G uy emerged from the back room and Clarice was on her feet before he reached the table. They shared a whisper and a laugh — "Did Moe say anything... Nope... So, how long since... Three years, easy..." — and then she was in the back room. She leaned over and kissed Gérard on the top of his head. Silent Moe poured her something from a different bottle — sherry, not brandy.

"So, when..."

"Husband or degree completion?"

"I'll leave the husband to your mother," Gérard said. "I was asking about your studies."

"Two credits to go — a few months."

"And then?"

Clarice had practiced her speech a dozen times in the three days since she had become aware of the information. There was no question in her mind that Gérard shared every bit of her father's chauvinism when it came to the idea of her becoming involved in the family business. At the same time, she also knew that Gérard was allowing the priest, an outsider, to care for his personal books and likely the books of the family — which meant that he was at least a little open to non-traditional thinking. But what she was counting on most was much more basic: that Gérard had never been known as someone to turn down a payday.

"It's simple," she said. "I have come into possession of some rather lucrative information."

Gérard stared back at her.

"Very lucrative information," Clarice said.

Gérard continued staring, and then he said, "You cannot. It's impossible."

"Listen for two minutes without interrupting. After that, if you want to pat me on the head and send me away, fine. I might have other options."

"It's inconceivable," Gérard said. "I mean, your father..."

"Two minutes," she said. "Two minutes, yes?"

The stare was harder this time. There was something on the old man's face that she couldn't quite decipher.

"Two minutes," he said, and then Gérard actually looked down at his watch. So did Silent Moe, from his seat in the outfield.

In the end, it didn't take 90 seconds. The information that she had obtained from one of her professors at the Sorbonne — a man with government connections — was that the French franc was about to be devalued. There was significant money to be made from this information, and it was a sure thing. The La Rue family profits would only be limited by the amount of money the family was willing to risk — and it wasn't a risk. The information was rock-solid.

Gérard was now leaning forward in his seat.

"Explain," he said. "Slowly."

Sometime in mid- to late-December, the franc would be devalued, she said. The country would make the announcement, and as if by magic, the amount of gold or foreign currency that a franc could purchase would be lowered by a certain percentage. From her information, that amount was likely about 15 percent.

"Why would they do such a thing?" Gérard said.

"It has to do with getting into the common market they're talking about with Europe and England," she said. "There's a need to, I don't know, equalize the values of the different currencies. You don't make them exactly equal, but get them in a kind of range of equality."

The old man nodded.

"OK, how does this help us?" he said.

Clarice went on to explain the basics of the futures markets when it came to currencies. You could place a bet, essentially, on whether you thought the value of the franc was going to go up or down during a specific time period.

"So you can bet it's going to go down?"

"Exactly," she said. "Except, in our case, it won't be gambling because we already know what's going to happen."

"And this is illegal?"

"Quite."

"So, how do you not get caught?"

"By placing your bets somewhere else," Clarice said. "You can't do it in the bourse here. You have to go to a foreign country, you have to use cash, and you have to pay off the broker you use to place the trade so that there is no paper trail."

"And this is doable? By whom?"

"By me, dear uncle. I suggest we do it in Zurich, where I have some connections because of school. I travel there with the money in my suitcase, and I make the arrangements, and I return after the devaluation with the profits. The guaranteed profits."

"Your suitcase? Really?"

"We could wire the money to an account, and I could withdraw it there, but why complicate things? The banks there are very secret when you want them to be, but why create a record when there is no need to create a record? Smuggling the money in and out is just neater and cleaner. I mean, have you ever seen any of the border guards open a single piece of luggage when you make the crossing? No less, a young girl's luggage?"

Clarice stopped talking. Gérard went from leaning forward to leaning back, arms folded, eyes closed. He sighed, and then he was quiet, and then he sighed again, deeper than the first time.

And then he leaned over his shoulder and said, "Maurice." Silent Moe came over, and Gérard whispered something in his ear. Then Gérard grabbed the pencil and notepad from his little side table, and scrawled something on it, and folded it, and handed it to Clarice. It was a larger amount than she had expected — not that she really expected anything.

"Come by the house in a few hours and Maurice will give you the money," Gérard said. "You will handle the investment as you see fit and keep 20 percent of the profit for yourself. The rest will be mine. This is my personal money, not La Rue money. This is a business arrangement between you and me and no one else is to know — not your father, not anyone. Understood?"

"Understood," Clarice said. "But there is another way to play this if you're willing to involve Martin. He makes a lot of foreign wine and liquor purchases, I believe. Well, if you told him to pre-pay some of his accounts, before the devaluation was announced, he would save a lot of money."

"No," Gérard said.

"But..."

"No. This is private, just between you and me. It has to be that way, and if you can't accept that, we're done with our two-minute conversation."

"No, no, I accept," Clarice said.

Gérard raised his glass, and Clarice raised hers. Gérard finished his, and Clarice barely wet her lips. She couldn't stand sherry.

Another kiss on the head, and they were done — except for Gérard placing his hands on Clarice's shoulders, and pushing her back a bit until they were just beyond nose-to-nose, and saying, "Don't let me down, baby girl."

PART II

MARKING THEIR TERRITORY

They had been drinking since it got dark, if you didn't count the beers at lunch. It had been that kind of a day, nothing much happening, just shit-talking and drinking. It was the kind of day that made Jerzy Lewinsky antsy, which is why he seemed to drink more than the rest of them. It was something he was aware of, too, the antsy-ness. "Self-medicating" is what he called it when he found himself downing three ryes to everyone else's two.

In the Levine family, Jerzy and his crew were known as the Young Bucks. As often as not, on days like that, they ended up in the informal Levine clubhouse, a big room in the back of a butcher shop off of Rue des Rosiers. The butcher had used it for cold storage at one point, apparently, but refrigeration had somehow reduced the amount of space they needed, and there had been a debt owed at some point, and the Levines ended up with a key to the back room, and a refrigerator of their own, and a card table, and a little bar — but it was such a shithole that mostly the Young Bucks used it. The older soldiers in the family had better places.

Jerzy was there that night with three of his crew members, and they were making fun of David Levine, the boss. It was what the Young Bucks did, especially when fueled by alcohol. They never mentioned Old Joe Levine when they got like this because they assumed that the technical boss of the family was pretty much a technical corpse at that point. David, his son, really ran things. David was the guy who took the envelope from Jerzy every month. David was the guy who always bitched about family standards not being met, and "rules and decorum" being important. David was the one who told Jerzy in their most recent conversation, "If I can smell the alcohol on your breath at 11 a.m., there's a problem. A big fucking problem."

"Because the envelope is light?" Jerzy said. Then he belched, and was fortunate that no one in the vicinity was lighting a match.

"The envelope isn't everything," David Levine said. "At some point, you know, a young buck has to grow up — because if he doesn't, if he doesn't start to observe the rules and decorum, if he doesn't start to take care, he ends up a dead buck."

Jerzy was reciting the speech to his boys, doing a bad imitation of David's deep baritone, and they were pissing themselves. Then, each in turn, they tried the imitation, and one was worse than the next, and the laughing was convulsive.

And with every fresh drink, the toast was the same:

"Young Bucks... Dead Bucks... Fuck it."

Jerzy could barely feel the tip of his nose when they locked the door behind them at the butcher shop. The rest had girlfriends to see, but Jerzy was free — "between snatches," as he told his mates. There was a regular bar a few blocks away, though, and he had some civilian friends who figured to be there — and, maybe some snatches. He figured he would stop for one more.

As it turned out, it was just two other guys he knew and no women. One more became two, and two became three, and Jerzy's fingertips were also becoming numb, and then one of the civilians said, "There's a new casino on Rue Pierre Dupont. Let's go check it out."

"Where did you say?" Jerzy said. His hearing was fine, but his attention span had shortened considerably through the evening.

"On Pierre Dupont."

"That's not possible."

"Fuck you — it's right there. I've seen it."

But it was not possible. Jerzy knew where Rue Pierre Dupont was, and while it was tucked into a corner of the 10th, it was clearly within the boundaries of the Levines' territory. Everybody knew the line between Levine territory and La Rue territory was Rue La Fayette. That was the line that had been brokered in the peace treaty. And if there was a new casino on Rue Pierre Dupont, it had to be a Levine casino — except that he knew there was no new Levine casino. He knew it because, while the Levines did do some casino work, David hated the casino business — "shitty people, shitty profits, not worth the effort." David said that as often as he said "rules and decorum."

And as they grabbed their coats, and one of the civilians got the bartender to call a taxi, Jerzy reached into his pocket. It was such a small pistol that sometimes he forgot about it, but it was there.

And 10 minutes after that, the three of them were piling out of the taxi. There was no sign out front of the building, just a gorilla bundled up against the cold. The gorilla asked what they wanted. One of the civilians said, "To try our luck in the best new place in town." The gorilla sneered but opened the door. They were drunk enough to be big losers and quick losers — that is, the best losers of all.

Inside, up one flight of steps, the casino was, in fact, there. Jerzy couldn't believe it. He looked around, and there were about a dozen punters in the place — three at the roulette table, five playing craps, the rest at a poker table. He could feel the heat rising in his face, even if his nose was numb. He put his hand in his coat pocket and fingered the revolver.

There was a bar along the far wall. It took Jerzy a second to focus, but he knew one of the bartenders. It was a La Rue kid who one of his crew once got into an argument with over a girl in a bar. It ended with a lot of fuck-you's and nothing worse.

A La Rue casino, then.

He fingered the gun and felt the safety.

This was a clear violation of the rules. The treaty had been brokered. The boundary was Rue La Fayette. This place was on the Levines' side of Rue La Fayette — just barely, maybe two blocks over, but it was definitely on the Levines' side.

Against the rules. Clearly fucking against the rules. The goddamn La Rues. They caused all of the trouble in the first place by grabbing both of the train stations when the Morels fell apart. Greedy fucking pigs. There should have been a negotiation from the beginning, and after they did what they did, there should have been an all-out war. Why David made peace after the Levines had them on the run — fucking pussy. It was what he thought when it happened and it was what he thought as he stood there.

With his thumb, Jerzy clicked off the safety. He did that, and he mumbled, "Fucking pussy."

This could not be allowed to stand. Rules and decorum insisted that it could not be allowed to stand.

Rules and decorum.

Fucking pussy.

Young Bucks... Dead Bucks...

"Fuck it!" Jerzy Lewinsky shouted, and then he said some other stuff while yanking the revolver out of his pocket. It caught on the fabric, though, and it took two yanks to get it out, and then Jerzy aimed the gun wildly toward the bar and squeezed the trigger.

The single bullet he fired lodged in the ceiling. The single bullet fired in reply lodged in his brain.

"Who the fuck is he?"

"Don't know."

"What did he say again?"

"'Who the hell do you La Rues think you are? There are rules to this arrangement.'"

"What does that mean?"

"Don't know."

"When do you tell the boss?"

"Not sure I have to."

"Freddy, I think you do."

"There won't be any publicity. No body for the cops to find. Not sure anybody outside of here has to know."

"Freddy, the boss would want to know."

"Yeah, maybe. It's late, though."

"Saturday night."

"Yeah, I was out with him earlier."

"Tomorrow, then."

"No, maybe Monday. No newspapers, no cops — there's no need to ruin Henri's weekend."

They bent over to drag the body off of the casino floor. The customers had long scattered, and the four of them were alone. When they turned the body over, they saw that one ear was partially blown off. Freddy stared at the face, though, and then observed, "Shit, he looks Jewish, doesn't he?"

S aturday night, like every Saturday night, was wives' night for the La Rue family. Henri wondered if it was like that for all of the families sometimes. He kind of liked David Levine — as much as you can like the operational head of a family who was trying to kill you not that long ago, and vice versa — but they almost never talked, and Henri never thought they were close enough for him to ask. You know, if Levine was wining and dining his side piece on Friday night and repeating the gesture for his wife on Saturday night. Come to think of it, he wasn't even sure if David Levine was married.

They tended to rotate the places, and this week was the Moulin Rouge. Henri hated the Moulin Rouge. He sometimes thought about putting his foot down and removing it from the rotation, but always backed off. Passy liked it because he was fucking one of the cigarette girls, and Passy was his right hand, and, well, the hell with it.

Still, that didn't mean he wouldn't bust Passy's balls about it.

They all had girlfriends, and their wives knew they all had girlfriends. They knew that, and they knew that Friday nights were reserved for the girlfriends, and they knew it from before they were married, and they accepted it. Accepted. The exact word. It was part of marriage to a gangster — fur coats, fancy vacations, Friday nights alone.

The cigarette girl was different, though. Both his wife (Carolina) and his girlfriend (Yvette) would have his nuts for lunch if they knew, for instance, that Passy once did the cigarette girl from behind in the alley while she was on her break — and while Carolina was out at the table watching the floor show.

That night was like most of them in that, after dinner, the women tended to cluster together toward the front of the table, nearest to the entertainment, while the men sat in the back and talked shop. At a certain point, Freddy and his wife begged off early — something about a babysitter problem, same as the week before. Then, Carolina was watching a juggler and then a comic and gabbing with Sylvie and the rest of the wives, while Passy bought his Gauloises from his girl, followed her into the back, and returned 10 minutes later with a barely suppressed smile.

"Well?" Henri said.

"Christ, really?"

"Yes, really."

"I finished on her face."

"Always the gentleman."

"She's redoing her makeup."

"As one must."

The two of them, old friends and old co-workers, burst out laughing — loud enough that Sylvie turned around and stared. Apparently, the comic was in the middle of a joke.

"Between you and me," Henri said.

"What?"

"We're not kids anymore. You going to be able to take care of Carolina when you get home?"

"Bah, separate rooms these days," Passy said.

"Because she's mad about—"

"Because she's mad about growing old is the best I can figure. I mean, whatever."

Henri shrugged and poured a couple more from the open bottle. The truth was, he and Sylvie were on an upswing in that department — not young and frisky like when they were in their twenties, but not dead and desiccated, either. It was all kind of nice. It is fair to say that theirs was a contentious marriage, but the two of them were partners, lifelong partners. She was a crucial business counselor for him, not only keeping her eyes and ears open when it came to the wives of his soldiers — the best source of information about their husbands — but also with a great sense of how to deal with Gérard. So there was that, and also, well, Sylvie's bitching in the background was, if not soothing like a concert played low on the radio, at least familiar. It was what he knew.

And then, with the sex lately, Henri smiled, and Passy caught him.

"What?"

"Nothing," Henri said. "Except the cigarette girl. I can't tell from here which side of her face she had to retouch."

O nly one of the four fountains at the Place des Vosges, which was about how it went. He'd never seen the full complement in operation, not in all of his years in Paris. One, two — that was normal. And the few times when he saw three, he thought it was a cause for celebration.

On this day, though, one. It wasn't too cold in the darkness, beneath the leafless trees and the dim street lights, and Jean Lemieux chose a bench with the wind at his back, and it wasn't too bad. The cassock and collar were back at the rectory. Lemieux wore what he sometimes called his Saturday clothes — dark brown slacks and shoes, camel-colored sport jacket, black overcoat. There was no getting away from that black garment, seeing as how it was the only warm coat he owned.

Lemieux came to Place des Vosges to think. It was not necessarily to examine his conscience, not like that, but just to close his eyes — or, sometimes, just have them go out of focus — and to inventory both his thoughts and his emotions.

On this day in mid-December, with the tree lights shining from dozens of windows all around him — the centuries-old apartment buildings that surrounded the square were owned by those well north of well-to-do on the economic scale — the out-of-focus tactic resulted in a gauzy kind of glow.

And, he thought: it's working.

And, he felt: then why am I so scared?

He watched Gérard closely and he could tell that he was succeeding. Slowly, slowly, the old man was crumbling. Part of him wished he didn't have to rely on his memory, but Lemieux did not dare keep a notebook. Besides, without photographs, well, photographs would be the best record of Gérard's decline — but there was no way to accomplish that.

So, the priest was stuck with his mental snapshots. Gérard's skin had gone from old and mottled — but still capable of pink cheeks on a cold day or after a brisk walk — to permanently sallow. After nine months of this, it was almost gray on some days — and he complained about hard patches on the soles of his feet besides. As for pink cheeks and brisk walks, they no longer existed. Gérard got himself to and from church in the morning, and out for lunch on Sundays, and that was about it.

Nine months. Good God. But it had to be that way. It had to be so gradual that it seemed natural, the decline. That part was working perfectly, and it would leave Gérard where Lemieux needed him to be when the next steps were taken.

Still, the priest worried. What if he was pushing things too far? What if he was miscalculating somehow? It wasn't as if he was trained to assess the old man. His eyes were not medically educated eyes, after all. There was no way to know what was going on inside Gérard's body. Lemieux saw how much bicarbonate he was drinking, and heard him say pretty much every day, "What I wouldn't give to take a solid shit." But the complaints were not increasing. It had been the same for at least four months. Gérard seemed to be slipping away very, very slowly. It was as if he was living on a hellish plateau with just the slightest downward tilt.

Another month.

Not much more.

Another month, and the next step.

Not much more.

Father Lemieux stood up and began wandering through the warren of streets that fed off of the Place de Vosges. He always arrived at the same destination after he'd had one of these conversations with himself, but he always took a different, meandering route. Left, right, left again — he didn't even think about it as he walked. His head was stuck where it had been stuck, worried but hopeful.

Another month.

Not much more.

"Ah, Mr. Morin — so good to see you," said the man who worked inside the door that he always managed to arrive at.

"Is Patrice available?" the priest said.

"Yes, yes, take a seat — won't be a minute."

———

Clarice had two boyfriends — not that she would ever tell her mother about either of them. Sylvie had stopped even asking because of the fights that followed every question. The fact that her mother took her father's side in the ongoing argument about working in the family business — that Sylvie seemed even more adamant about it than Henri, somehow — caused the rupture that was unbridgeable, at least from Clarice's perspective. The way the daughter had the relationship figured, her mother neither loved her nor liked her. Worst of all, her mother was jealous of her — the education, the potential, all of it. She was jealous of her daughter and she felt threatened by her.

During their most recent fight, Sylvie had yelled, "You can have influence. You just have to do it behind the scenes. There is power in whispering."

"So, why are you screaming?"

"You know what I mean."

"I do know," Clarice said. "You and your whispers. You don't have the balls to be at the table. You hide behind your own skirts. You're afraid of the risks. You're afraid to be heard by more than one man. Afraid to make your own way. Afraid to be rejected. Afraid of the consequences. Afraid. It is no way to live."

After that one, Clarice began spending even less time at the family house in Montmartre and more time near the Sorbonne — on the couch of one of her girlfriends, or with one of her boyfriends. There were two of them.

One of them was her age. Pierre. He was a graduate student in history, which left him with decidedly dismal prospects when measured in francs. That didn't matter, though, because Clarice and Pierre didn't talk about the future — not a him-and-her future, anyway. They were buddies more than lovers — although the sex was an integral part of their relationship, especially the thing that Pierre did with his finger. For the two of them, Saturdays were for lying around naked all day. They only left his tiny apartment to eat.

When they weren't fucking, they were laughing and arguing and existing so comfortably. They would have had a future if he hadn't been Jewish, a reality that would have sent both sets of parents into the kind of state that often resulted in not only screaming, but also cutting off financial support. And that couldn't happen, especially not for Pierre.

Then there was Clarice's other man. Louis. He was a professor of economics and finance. He was as old as Henri and had a daughter exactly Clarice's age. His family lived outside the city and he kept a pied-à-terre where he slept most weeks during the semester from Monday to Thursday. Sometimes, he would come to the city on Sunday afternoon "to grade these goddamn papers." Those were the Sundays when Clarice missed lunch at Vincent's. When she was still bothering to inform her mother, she sometimes said she was going to see her "girlfriend" on Thursday night to start the weekend early. Louis on Thursday. Pierre on Friday and Saturday. Louis on Sunday.

The sex with Louis was great, too, but she was the aggressor. With them, it was her finger that did the work. And as it turned out, the old man had more stamina that she expected, and memorable equipment besides.

It was after a second go-round one Thursday night — he was leaning on an elbow and smoking a cigarette, she was washing her hands in the basin — when Louis told her about the drink he'd had the previous week with an old school chum, now a fairly senior official in the ministry of finance. During the conversation, the friend explained about the upcoming devaluation of the franc. Louis actually whispered when he told her.

A fter the mini-war against the Levines over the train stations — that is, after Willy and his men were slaughtered in the office that fronted on the Place de la République, slaughtered by the Levines — Freddy was put in charge of the Gare du Nord. It was a significant promotion for Henri's youngest lieutenant — other than his son — but he made the most sense. Among other things, Freddy was by far the handiest La Rue man when it came to the use of any and all firearms. His predecessor had been a genius of organization — but, as Passy said, "Look where all of those neatly kept ledgers got our Willy. His brains were blown all over his perfect fucking penmanship."

So, if Freddy was a little young and a little scattered, Henri figured he could mentor him and that the kid would grow into the job. Boys became men in their thirties, Henri believed, and he would guide Freddy and maybe accelerate the process. It was going well, too. The envelopes were of the appropriate weight, and the headaches seemed to be nothing beyond the usual bullshit of their business: cops who suddenly materialized with their hands out, employees who drank too much or spent too much time with their pants around their ankles, stuff like that. Freddy was dealing with the headaches after seeking some advice from Henri — and so, a fatter envelope for this cop, a backhand and a threat for this young lunkhead on the staff. Henri had been attentive at the start — or, as Freddy said to him, "so far up my fucking ass" — but the boss had begun to back off in recent months.

It really felt like the La Rue operation in their half of the 10th arrondissement was humming. The truth was, the whole thing was humming. The traditional La Rue base was in Montmartre (the 18th) and below it in the 9th, and there hadn't been a hiccup there in forever. Guy was working out better than his father ever expected with his two brothels, and Timmy and Passy kept Trinity One operating like a goddamned printing press for francs. They had been in charge for more than a decade — Passy of the Trinity One casino, Timmy of the brothel one flight above — and the returns were big and consistent. It was safer than owning a bond in Électricité de France. Every month, the La Rues clipped the fucking coupon and collected.

Henri knew less about Martin's end of the business, the liquor, and knew almost nothing about Michel's heroin trade. Well, he knew the profit-sharing envelope he received every quarter, and it too was consistent and growing. The whole thing seemed too easy sometimes.

"I had just said to Passy, 'It's been too quiet, some shit is coming.' Goddammit, Freddy. God-fucking-dammit."

They were in the back room of the uniform company on Avenue de Clichy. It was the legitimate arm of the La Rue family, a company that made school uniforms. It existed to break even — which it did, barely — and to provide pay stubs to everyone under Henri's purview, so as to keep the tax authorities happy. Passy ran the thing — a complete pain in the ass, but a fair trade-off for the huge income he received from Trinity One. Henri kept an office — his only office — in the back.

It was Monday morning, and Freddy had arrived with the

news of the punter who ended up dead on his casino floor on Saturday night.

"Who—"

"I did," Freddy said.

"Of course you fucking did."

"Boss, he took a shot at one of my guys working the bar."

"Which guy?"

"Tommy."

"Fuck me. The one who—"

"Yeah, drank too much and spent too much time sniffing his fingers. But I took care of that, like you said. He's been good. He was just working the bar, minding his own business."

"And which casino was this? Wait a minute."

It just dawned on Henri that the La Rues were no longer in the casino business in the 10th, that the Levines had taken the single shitty joint in the arrondissement as part of the deal that split up the train stations.

"Freddy," Henri said. He wasn't screaming anymore. His was snarling, quietly.

"Boss, it was perfectly legitimate."

"The fuck it was. Nothing's legitimate if I don't know about it. Motherfucker. How long?"

"Two weeks."

"Babysitter problems, my ass."

"It's been good," Freddy said, desperate to steer the conversation toward the envelopes.

"It can't be good if I didn't know about it," Henri said. He was yelling again. He couldn't believe how often he found himself repeating the Uncle Gérard line about how "hogs get slaughtered." He always made fun of Gérard for that behind his back, and sometimes to his face.

"I was just trying to show some initiative," Freddy said.

"Fuck you and fuck your initiative. So where exactly is this shithole?"

Freddy told him it was on Rue Pierre Dupont, and Henri opened the door to the office and walked over to the enormous map of the city that was tacked up outside. The uniform delivery people used it in setting up their routes.

Henri looked around, and everyone — Passy at his desk, the seamstresses, all of them — had their eyes down and were concentrating on what was in front of them, or pretending to concentrate.

Henri checked the map again, squinting, just to be sure. Then he slammed the door and screamed, "On the other side of Rue La Fayette?"

Freddy nodded.

"What makes you think…"

"It's in the agreement, Henri. It's completely legitimate."

"The hell it is. It's on the other side of Rue La Fayette."

"It's legit."

"Bullshit."

"You made the deal, and you explained it to us. It's legitimate. I swear. I wouldn't have done something to violate the agreement. Henri, I swear."

Henri's mind immediately went back to the peace treaty that he and David Levine had negotiated that day, sitting on a bench in Montmartre Cemetery. It's not as if anybody wrote anything down, but the understanding seemed clear enough to Henri. The big part of the deal was the division of the train stations — the bigger and more lucrative Gare du Nord to the La Rues, the Gare de l'Est to the Levines. The La Rues took the two crappy whorehouses that were more trouble than they were worth. The Levines got the crappy casino that also was more a pain in the ass than anything.

Then Freddy began talking.

"I can repeat that conversation word for word — that's how meaningful it was to me," he said. And then he did repeat it, word for word, and Henri listened to his recitation. Train stations, check. Brothels, check. Casino, check.

"Then, the street money," Freddy said. "You said that the Levines wanted it all, but that you negotiated a split. The dividing line for the street money was Rue La Fayette."

"Like I said," Henri said.

"The dividing line for the street money — that was it," Freddy said. "There was no dividing line for anything else, right? There was no mention of a dividing line before you came to the street money, right? Boss, I listened. It was the first big conversation I'd ever been a part of, and I listened. It's fucking imprinted on my memory. The Rue La Fayette line was about street money and only street money. That's how you explained it. Am I wrong?"

Henri closed his eyes and rubbed his temples and thought back to Montmartre Cemetery. And when he did, he realized that Freddy was right, and that there was indeed a loophole in the deal, and that the little fucker had jumped through it with both feet.

"Boss," Freddy said, and Henri opened his eyes. Freddy explained that there were no police and no newspapers that night. He said that the customers in the place were all in the wind, which wasn't ideal. That included the two guys who came in with the dearly departed, which was even less ideal.

Henri said nothing. His head suddenly seemed full of static.

"There's one more thing, Boss," Freddy said. "Tommy looked at the dead guy and, well, he's not 100 percent sure — I mean, I got him in the head after he took the shot at Tommy, and it was kind of messy."

"But..."

"Not 100 percent, but Tommy thinks the stiff looked like a

Levine guy who was there this one time when he got in a beef over a girl."

At which point, the static cleared — or, rather, morphed. Because what Henri was feeling then was his heart beginning to beat faster, and an overall ache in his gut.

PART III

INITIATION

Clarice bought herself a spot in a first class compartment on the early morning train from Gare de l'Est to Zurich. It was a seven-hour trip overall, with a long stop in Strasbourg and a change of trains in Basel. That was where the customs business would happen, on the platform in Basel.

It was going to be a five-night visit, based on her prediction of the timing of the announcement of the devaluation by the French treasury. It almost certainly had to be over the weekend, when the markets were closed. Her guess was that it would be on the morning of December 28th, a Sunday. The franc would collapse as the markets opened on Monday morning, and Clarice would collect her profit and be on the noon train back to Paris, the suitcase significantly heavier than when she had arrived. If Louis was right about the devaluation, it would be 100 times heavier, give or take.

So, she was traveling out of Paris on Christmas Eve morning. The battle with her mother over that particular scheduling arrangement was epic. It lasted for the better part of two days, and only came off the roiling boil when Clarice hinted about a boy from school she was visiting. Which was bullshit.

The date just made too much sense, for a couple of reasons. One was that she needed to be ready to do business early on Friday morning, the 26th. That one day was her only window. If she missed it, she failed. So, there was that, and there also was the reality that the train would be a circus on Christmas Eve. The circus would help the young woman in first class traveling with a purse that held 530,000 French francs — 500,000 of Gérard's and 30,000 of Guy's; their little secret. There was no way that any border guard would be opening suitcases or purses from the insistent menagerie on the platform, all of them loaded with Christmas presents and worried about getting to Mass on time.

So Clarice felt oddly relaxed when she eased into her compartment, already full with a husband, wife and two children. She was polite for five minutes — not six — and then closed her eyes. It was the same as it had been for the previous week. In the darkness, the numbers just kept bouncing off of each other:

500,000 French francs

1-to-100 margin requirements

17.55 percent devaluation

58,775,000 French francs on the other end

That was all for Gérard. As for Guy, his 30,000 would grow to more than 3,000,000.

There would be expenses, certainly. The commission and the rest of whatever might be needed to grease the open palms along the way might knock it down to closer to 50,000,000 francs. But, still. And based on the deal with Uncle Gérard, 10,000,000 of that would be hers — more than enough to go out on her own if her mother and father still insisted on keeping her out of the La Rue family business. But how could they — unless Gérard insisted on keeping the whole thing a secret.

The train ride was uneventful. The border control festivities in Basel were as she predicted — a complete zoo. The guard stamped her passport without even looking at her or the picture. And the money in her purse — that was never an issue.

Christmas dinner alone in a foreign country was a little weird, but really not so bad. The 9 a.m. appointment she had made with Gerhard Richter began at precisely 9:01. Richter was glad to see her again, but he seemed concerned as Clarice explained the purpose of her visit. It would mean big money to him, and Richter knew it. But it would be against the rules of the Zurich exchange, and he knew that, too. The concern on his face, though, seemed more like constipation. He wanted to get there, but was struggling...

"I don't know," he said. It was about the fifth time he'd said it in 15 minutes.

"You don't know what?"

"It's a lot, a lot of contracts."

"With all due respect, that's bullshit and you know it. Your firm alone probably does 10 times that number of contracts in a day, just on the French franc."

"Maybe not 10."

"What, nine times as many?" Clarice said. "All of those companies hedging their exposure. The ones selling wine going one way, worried that the Swiss francs they're getting will decrease in value. The ones selling precision machine tools going the other way, worried that the French franc they're getting will go down. You taking a slice of every transaction. You know it as well as I do. It's more than 10 times as many contracts."

"Well, maybe 10."

They talked some more about the mechanics of the thing, about hiding Clarice's transactions amid others on the firm's books. They talked about how she needed the standard margin agreement, and how settlement would have to come quickly after the devaluation announcement, the next trading day. They talked mostly about how her name could not be on a single piece of paper, not anywhere.

"Completely off the books," she said. "Absolutely, totally, completely."

"No banks?"

"God, no."

"But..."

"No banks, no need," Clarice said.

At which point, she removed the bundle from her purse, the bundle containing the 50 Bonapartes of Gérard's money and the three Bonapartes of Guy's money, and tossed it onto the blotter on Richter's desk. They both just kind of stared at the Bonaparte that was on the top of the stack, the 10,000 franc bill that most people didn't see very often, the one where the general is kind of peering over his right shoulder at the Arc de Triomphe.

After which, she came around to where Richter was sitting and slowly undid the buttons behind which lay the little friend she first met as a university sophomore on a six-week internship. She met him the first time near the end of the second week, behind the very same desk, and about three days a week thereafter.

By the time she was redoing the buttons, Richter had agreed to a five percent commission on the back end — more than 3,000,000 francs, give or take. It was lower than his firm's standard fee, but seeing as how the whole thing was going to be off the books, it was more than worth it to him. If Clarice had to guess, it would be worth four or five years' salary for one of the highest paid brokers in Zurich.

F ather Lemieux's time with Patrice was as it always was. He went to her every time, maybe a dozen times a year for going on four years. The whole thing usually took about 20 minutes. The first 10 involved undressing and sharing a drink. The rest involved Patrice verbally abusing the priest while he physically pounded her. Her insults tended to center on the size of his dick — he knew, from the seminary showers, that it was entirely average, but she had experienced bigger and demeaned him by comparison. There was that, and also the overall lack of tone of his body — skinny but soft, the muscles entirely undefined. Mostly, though, there was his chosen profession and the shame he must have been feeling as he screwed her. Every time,

Patrice managed to work in the same phrase: "God's hollow little man with the sad little peen."

Within minutes, every time, he was done — pounding her from behind, staring at the back of her head, listening as she shouted insults at the headboard. He had never asked for the insults. They were just her thing, delivered on her own initiative and starting with the first night. He sometimes wondered if he would be quite as fucked up in the head if the first whore he had been with had been someone other than Patrice, someone sweet or solicitous or protective. But Jean Lemieux never changed whores and never found out.

There was a quiet little bar off of the lobby, and that was where Lemieux had his meetings with one particular individual. Alain Benneville was already seated at a small corner table, and the priest brought them two cognacs from the bar.

"Doctor," Lemieux said.

"Father."

"Did you, uh, partake?"

"When in Rome," Benneville said, and they toasted wordlessly to whatever — being in Rome, perhaps.

Benneville was a general practitioner who always impressed Lemieux as a bit of an operator. The priest and the doctor had first met a decade earlier when Lemieux was a young assistant pastor at St. Genevieve's and Benneville was the chairman of a fundraising drive to renovate the basement sanctuary that the parish used for its Sunday children's Mass. They started as professional friends, but their relationship grew over the years, even after Lemieux was transferred to his current job, overseeing the archdiocese's books for the cardinal. They both enjoyed a drink and, as it turned out in the last couple of years, they both were a little flexible about the meaning of the vows they had taken — Lemieux to the church, Benneville to his wife. Benneville had been the one who suggested the brothel, and was the only one who knew Lemieux's secret besides Patrice and the guy working the door. And, as the doctor said, "Don't fucking worry about them — in their business, it's like the confessional is in your business." The priest liked to believe that it was true.

Benneville also was the only one who knew about his intentions with Gérard. That is, Lemieux told him about how the old man had grasped onto him as more than a clerical friend, and how Lemieux had decided that there might be some real value in the relationship — but that the true value could not be unlocked without Lemieux being able to take another step closer to Gérard and the family. Keeping an eye on the old man's ledgers was one thing, but being involved in the financial decision-making was different. That step closer was where the money would be for the priest.

And, when Lemieux told him what he hoped to do, it was Dr. Benneville who replied with a single word: "arsenic."

That had been nearly a year earlier. Now, when they met — pretty much monthly in the little brothel bar — the doctor asked the priest the same series of questions in pretty much the same order.

"Complexion?" Benneville said.

"Gray. Same. No worse than a few months ago."

"Skin overall?"

"Gray, like I said. And now he's complaining about a wart on the sole of one of his feet. Left foot, I think."

"Energy level?"

"He's always kind of tired."

"Digestive stuff?"

"Same as it's been lately. Farting all the time. Always on the toilet, from what he says. Gérard's favorite phrase lately is 'like shit through a goose.' And he says he throws up occasionally."

"Appetite?"

"Meh. But, he eats."

"No heart issues yet?"

"He hasn't mentioned it."

"You're sure?"

"He hasn't mentioned it."

"How about shortness of breath?"

"Nope."

"Chest pain?"

"Nope."

"Dizziness?"

"Not that I've seen," Father Lemieux said. "We walk from his house to Sacré Coeur every morning — you've seen how far it is, just up the block. A five-minute walk that takes more than 10 minutes, but that's it. His balance is fine. He doesn't have much stamina, but no dizziness."

"That's the one I worry about — the chest pain, the shortness of breath, the dizziness from low blood pressure. You're sure?"

"Pretty sure."

The doctor took a sip of the cognac. It was the same questions every month — only Benneville's tone that was changing.

"Well, if he does — chest pain, dizziness, like that — it's a borderline emergency," he said. "The first hint of that, you'll need to stop immediately. And I really think, well, you should probably stop now anyway. I mean, he might surprise you and go to a doctor if he's feeling as bad as you make it out."

"He's never going to the doctor. That's the only thing I'm sure of."

"But, why can't you stop now?" the doctor said.

"A couple of weeks more, that's all," the priest said.

There had been one bundle of Bonapartes in her purse when she crossed the border into Basel five days earlier. There were now 116 bundles of Bonapartes in her suitcase, along with only her underwear. She'd had to ditch the rest of her clothes and shoes to make room.

The bag was heavy but not crazy-heavy — really, barely heavier than when it had been packed with the dresses and shoes and toiletries. She could lift it easily and carry it a goodly distance, but she didn't. That's what taxi drivers and train station porters were for, and that's what a well-to-do young woman traveling in first class would do — use a porter. So, that's what Clarice did when the train from Basel reached Strasbourg — pointed at the next porter lined up at the door of the first class carriage.

The walk to the security control area was about 200 feet. It was located at the end of the platform. There were three border guards working at three tables, and Clarice chose the youngest of the three, even though his line was a bit longer than the others. By her reckoning, the guard was under 30 and handsome besides.

"How long were you in Switzerland?" he said. He had barely looked at her before thumbing through the passport.

"Five days."

"Business or pleasure."

"Pleasure," she said, "if visiting a hard-of-hearing aunt and a flatulent uncle for Christmas can be considered a pleasure."

The border guard looked up, and he made eye contact, and he smiled.

"What's your destination?"

"Paris, but I'm often in Strasbourg," Clarice said, and this time she was the one who initiated the eye contact, and she was the one who smiled.

The border guard asked where she stayed when she was in the city, and Clarice named the only hotel she knew, the Gutenberg, because she had seen it out of the train window. Clarice asked where he worked, and the border guard said, "Nine to five, Monday to Friday, right here."

They both smiled again.

He said, "Well, until the next time," and then the border guard stamped Clarice's passport, and the porter carried her unexamined bag onto the next train to the Gare de l'Est.

***

The only time Freddy had been to The Onyx, it had been strictly business. After the Levines had killed Willy and his crew as a protest against the La Rue family takeover of both of the train stations in the 10th, the La Rues decided that there needed to be some retribution. A younger Levine family soldier was identified, and his favorite haunt — The Onyx, where the dancers were all black, as were a majority of the customers — was where Freddy was dispatched to deliver the La Rues' reply. It was a shot to the head, as Freddy remembered it, but he couldn't believe he wasn't entirely sure. What he did remember precisely, though, was that a girl was blowing the Levine soldier in one of the line of little rooms in the back when Freddy began blasting.

Within seconds, Freddy was out the back door of the place and in the wind. It was a perfect bit of business, flawless — until the La Rues found out that the dead soldier had impregnated one of David Levine's daughters, and that they had been married in a private ceremony the previous week. Besides the embarrassment of the publicity, what started as soldier-to-soldier retribution escalated into a soldier-to-family thing. Not good.

The deal between the Levines and La Rues remade the peace, though, with the La Rues forfeiting the Gare de l'Est. But the symbolism of The Onyx still meant something to everyone, it appeared.

Or, as Freddy screamed at Tiny, "The fucking Onyx? It had to be the fucking Onyx? You can get blown in a thousand different places in this town. The best brothels, the stinkiest alleys, a fucking thousand. And you had to go to The Onyx?"

"What can I say?" Tiny said.

"But—"

"It's what I like," Tiny said. They called him Tiny because he was six foot five.

"Ease up, Freddy — a man likes what he likes," Timmy said. The three of them were sitting in the bar of the brothel at Trinity One. It was, by reputation, the classiest whorehouse in Paris and just a flight of steps away from the most discriminating casino in Paris.

Passy ran the casino for the La Rue family and Timmy ran the brothel. Passy was meticulous about the money and Timmy was even more meticulous about the girls. A girl did not get hired — could not get hired — until the man himself was sure of their quality, which could only be ascertained after a thorough inspection. When they talked about it, Passy and Timmy always devolved into the same comedy routine with the same concluding lines.

Timmy: "Each and every one of them has my seal of approval on her ass."

Passy: "Among other things."

Timmy: "To each his own."

Earlier that night, Tiny had been to The Onyx, and had taken his favorite girl — a five-foot-nothing bleach blonde — into one of the little rooms off of the back corridor. He was sitting on the little cot, and the girl was on her knees, and the purpose of the evening was proceeding as it typically did when the curtain flew open. Occupied with other matters, it took Tiny a half-second to react to the man pointing a revolver at him, but he did react. He was in the process of flinging himself down and to the left when the shot was fired. At least, he thought he had started moving before the shot but he wasn't sure. Whatever happened, the gunman missed Tiny. He missed badly — so badly that the only person hit was the bleach blonde, right in the back of the head.

"The guy panicked and ran," Tiny said. "I grabbed my shit and ran after him, but it took me a few seconds to get my pants up. I had a gun in my jacket, but he must have gone left out of the back alley when I went right."

"And nobody saw you?" Freddy said.

"Everybody saw me — I'm six fucking five."

"That was going in. But not after?"

"No, not after," Tiny said.

The three of them had another drink from the cognac bottle that sat nearly empty on their table. Timmy poured, and they all sipped, and then he said, "Well, there is a kind of poetic justice to the whole thing."

"Yeah, well..." Freddy said.

"Kind of like rhyming couplets."

"Fuck poetry," Freddy said.

He knew what Timmy was saying, though. The La Rues had sought revenge in that back corridor of The Onyx, and now the Levines had sought revenge in the same place after the killing of their man at Freddy's new casino on Rue Pierre Dupont.

They were all quiet for a few seconds — maybe as long as a minute — when Timmy said what they were all thinking.

"Henri's gonna shit," he said.

"As long as he doesn't shit on me," Freddy said.

"Might think about wearing high boots when you tell him," Timmy said.

"Really, you think?"

"Waders," Timmy said. "Like for duck hunting."

Freddy knew that Timmy was right. He had tried to convince Henri that the whole thing would blow over — that there wasn't even a body, and there had been no cops or newspapers, and that the friends would be too scared to talk — and besides, the dead guy had fired first and for no reason.

"Un-fucking-provoked" was the term that Freddy used in his recitation with his boss. He used it a dozen times, maybe more. But Henri had remained unconvinced — and now this.

"It's still like it's fucking Christmas week — tomorrow is New Year's Eve," Freddy said. "I think it can wait a day or two. I mean, nobody got hurt. You know, except…"

"It's going to be in the papers," Timmy said.

"With no connection to us," Freddy said.

"Unless somebody fingers your big lunkhead with a taste for the dark meat," Timmy said.

He looked at Tiny.

"No offense," Timmy said. "A man likes what he likes."

"But it's not like anybody knows your name, right?" Freddy said.

Tiny shook his head and said, "Not such a lunkhead."

"Again, no offense," Timmy said.

Freddy and Timmy — they were equals on the family organizational chart, but Timmy had 20 years more experience in the business — talked through some possible eventualities. As the two of them schemed, Tiny grabbed the bottle and tried to drink himself into a stupor. At his size, that would take some doing, and he wasn't close to drunk when Freddy stood up and told him he would drive him home.

Then, as they were walking away, Timmy grabbed Tiny by

the arm and said, "So, like, right in the middle of sucking you off?"

"Yeah."

"And when the shot was fired?"

"Yeah, what?"

"Well, did she, like, bite it?"

"No, she just kind of fell."

"Well, I guess that's good to know," Timmy said.

———————

Gérard was returning from what he counted as his seventh trip to the toilet that day. It was just past 8 p.m., and Maurice was just leaving for dinner at home with his wife when the doorbell rang. It was Clarice. She was lugging a suitcase along with her.

"Maurice," Gérard said, indicating that he should carry it. But Clarice breezed past him and into the living room. Gérard shrugged, and Silent Moe left to get his dinner.

"Straight from the station?" Gérard said.

"Seemed the best idea."

"And no one..."

"No one knows," Clarice said.

It was a small fib. Guy knew, but Clarice knew that she could trust her brother. She knew because there were roughly 3,500,000 reasons for him to keep the whole thing to himself.

In the taxi, she had transferred Guy's share of the Bonapartes to her purse, seven stacks. That left 109 stacks in the suitcase for her and Gérard to divide — about 87 for him and 22 for her. She had decided to have him do the dividing.

It took about a minute to pile the stacks of Bonapartes on the table next to Gérard's chair. As she built the pyramid, she took two different peeks at the old man's face. The skin was still gray, and he still looked like shit overall. But his eyes were wider and brighter than she had remembered, and a smile was just plastered on his face.

"How many?"

"One hundred and nine. But you need to count."

"Please, you're my niece, I certainly trust you."

"It's business," Clarice said. "Count."

As he worked his way through the money, her uncle kept muttering through the smile. He got to 50 stacks and stopped for a second, and he looked at her, and he said, "I mean, I did believe in you. But, this..."

Gérard went back to counting.

"One hundred and nine," he said.

"Good."

He began picking stacks off of the top of the pile, and she counted as he counted.

"That's 25 for you," her uncle said.

"Should be just under 22."

"A bonus."

"No, really."

"A bonus," Gérard said. "A well-deserved bonus."

He got to his feet and walked over to the small bar.

"Sherry?" he said.

"Uncle, I hate sherry."

"Well, what?"

"Same as you're having."

"Two cognacs, then," he said.

Again, there was the smile as he poured. She saw that, and she smiled, too. She knew that she had impressed her uncle. She felt it deeply, too, even as she kept running the numbers through her head. For his investment of 500,000 francs, Gérard now had 42,000,000 and she had 12,500,000. It spent the same way in France, even after the devaluation. And if they ever wanted to changed it into, say, American dollars at the new rate, Gérard's was worth about $10,000,000, hers about $3,000,000, and Guy's a little shy of $1,000,000.

He smiled, she smiled. He sipped, she sipped. And then the uncle said to the niece, "Sit — we have a few things to discuss."

———

The invitation to drinks at Gérard's at 3 p.m. on New Year's Eve was a command performance, and the invitees — Henri, Martin and Michel — were all in place in the old man's living room. Silent Moe and Father Lemieux also were there, with Moe serving as bartender.

"So, what's up?" Henri said.

"Don't know," Lemieux said.

"Gotta be something."

"Not just a friendly New Year's drink?"

"I thought priests were supposed to know how to read people," Henri said. Then he kind of half snorted and walked away.

Just then, the door opened and Gérard entered the living room with Clarice on his arm. Martin and Michel looked at Henri as a kind of reflex — she was his daughter, after all — and he just shrugged. The priest leaned in and said, "See, just a family day," and Henri froze him in mid-sentence with a stare.

"Sit, sit," Gérard said. The chairs had been organized in a semi-circle around him, as they tended to be for family meetings. None of them had noticed the extra chair for Clarice.

"I have a story to tell you all," Gérard said, at which point he laid out the tale of the devaluation of the franc — how Clarice had brought it to him, and how she had conceived of the plan, and how she had managed the execution. The only part he left out was how she blew Gerhard Richter as a part of the commission negotiations, and that was only because she hadn't told him.

When he was done, Gérard took a sip and said, "Maurice," and Silent Moe walked over to join the group. Gérard had five envelopes on his table. He handed the two thinnest to Silent Moe and Father Lemieux. Each of theirs contained 500,000 francs.

"A gesture of my thanks and my affection," Gérard said. "And now, if you'll please leave us."

When they were gone, Gérard handed the three bulging manila envelopes to Henri, Martin and Michel.

"I'm kicking up to you — or, rather, kicking down," their uncle said. "I'm under no obligation, mind you. It was all my risk. Although, with this girl, there was no risk."

Clarice had determined not to show any emotion, and this was the hardest moment, but she succeeded. No smile, no nothing — just as blank an expression as she could manage.

"There's 2,000,000 francs in there for each of you," Gérard said. "Real money, yes? Real money, all due to the brains and the initiative shown by Henri's daughter here."

He stopped, sipped.

"Now, as the head of this family, here is what I propose," Gérard said. And then he laid out what he and Clarice had discussed two nights earlier. They would all forego their next quarterly payment from the pot, a total of about 5,000,000 francs. That would be Clarice's investment stake. Her charge was a big one: to earn a 50 percent return on that money every three months.

"Fifty, really?" she said.

"Yes, really."

"It's not like you can make that much legally in the stock market, or at least not very often. And it's not like they devalue the franc every day."

"I didn't say legal, I said 50 percent," Gérard said, and Clarice eventually agreed. The terms of her employment were simple enough: an annual salary of 500,000 francs — "It's about what Guy earns, and I think that's fair for a 23-year-old in this family," Gérard said — and half of all profits above 50 percent.

"That's it," Gérard told the semi-circle. "Every three months, the profits go into the pot for distribution and Clarice is left with the same 5,000,000 to work her magic. As she said, the amount is big enough to be meaningful without being so big as to draw undue attention. I think that's smart, but I guess we can revisit it after a few quarters."

As Gérard spoke, everyone was sneaking peeks at Henri. He had made no secret about not wanting Clarice in the family business. The Guy thing had been tough enough, but he seemed even more adamant about his daughter. Clarice sneaked a couple of peeks at him, too, and this one time, he caught her. Their eyes locked until she turned away, but she could see in that brief glance that he was pre-volcanic. Gérard saw it, too — they all must have.

"It's my decision and it's been made," Gérard said. "Henri, you need to make peace with this. Your girl is too big of an asset to squander. If you don't want to participate, I guess we could work something out with your quarterly share of the pot. But I really don't want to do that. This is happening, with or without you. I'm still in a position to make this decision and I'm making it. It's for the good of the family — the whole family. But I want you to be with me on it, to be with us."

Gérard looked at Henri and saw that his nephew had been completely blindsided. That had been the plan — as he had told Clarice, "an essential part of the plan."

He had told her, "Look, it's not my place to get between a father and his daughter, and I don't think I'm doing that. I think I'm building a bridge instead. But, honestly, that's secondary.

You'll learn this quickly enough, but my job is to be the steward of the family business, and you need to be a part of it — and you just brought back about 55,000,000 reasons why."

The meeting was over when Gérard finished speaking. Martin and Michel didn't know what to do, other than cradle their cash and wish Clarice well with a kiss on both cheeks. Henri did not participate in the well-wishing. He just turned and left the house, carrying his bulging manila envelope.

PART IV

A NEW FACE

They had talked about it all through their New Year's Eve dinner at Maxim's, and as they sat around the apartment on New Year's Day, and then the next day, too. Henri and Sylvie ping-ponged between being angry and being philosophical about the Clarice situation. As Sylvie dressed for a lunch out with some girlfriends, Henri sat on the edge of the bed and felt his emotions continue to twist his innards, even two days after the scene in Gérard's living room.

"I mean, fucking Gérard—"

"He's a devious old shit," Sylvie said.

"You seem impressed."

"I honestly didn't think he still had it in him."

"But, I mean, you were against Clarice getting into the business even more than I was."

"I was and I am," Sylvie said. "But it's done, right? There's no way to counteract it or countermand it. The money's too big — and you know that it's big enough that you'd be outvoted by the rest of them if it ever came to that."

"It's not a democracy."

"It's just money."

"The franc is our leader, always has been," Henri said.

He changed position, from sitting to reclining on the bed, his fingers laced behind his head. Sylvie was dressing pretty well for a run-of-the-mill Saturday lunch with Passy's wife and a few of the others. The perfume was her Saturday night perfume. The dress was just a bit much for the afternoon.

She fixed her hair in the mirror and caught Henri's eye in the reflection.

"Isn't part of you at least a little bit proud?" Sylvie said.

"I guess."

"No, really."

"Yeah, I'm proud," he said. "I'm proud, I'm stunned, I'm

pissed off. I didn't know you could be all of those things at the same time, but there you have it."

They talked some more about the bulging manila envelope, and how they might spend it. Henri mentioned a new car. Sylvie mentioned a new living room suite. Both of them talked about a new roof for the house in Normandy. There was enough for all of that and more, a lot more.

They talked and wondered if Clarice had spent her last night under their roof. Henri had no idea what her commission on the deal had been, but he figured it had been big — a lot bigger than what was in his envelope. If she had been smart enough to concoct the whole scheme, she was smart enough to get a fair piece for herself. She hadn't been home since the New Year's Eve meeting with Gérard, and they guessed she was checking out apartments as they sat there. Probably office space, too.

"We're going to have to talk to her," Henri said.

"Congratulate her?" Sylvie said.

"What's the alternative?"

"A Cold War forever."

"You can hold a grudge with the best of them, my love, but against Clarice? I don't think so,"

"Yeah," Sylvie said.

Long pause. Flick of the hair.

"Yeah," she said.

"I mean, she's in the business but not really. It's a different thing. A lot of it might end up being legitimate. Might not be the worst thing."

"You sound like you're trying to convince yourself."

"So, how am I doing?" Henri said.

He watched his wife as they talked, and Sylvie tried on three different necklaces before deciding on the most expensive one, a diamond pendant on a platinum chain, a present for their 10th anniversary. And as he got more used to the idea of Clarice, his mind jumped to his wife, and how the whole lunch-with-the-girls thing had to be bullshit.

But who was the man?

It wasn't Jack Quillette — that was for sure. Quillette was the La Rues' butcher, and Henri was somewhere between pretty sure and positive that he had been fucking Sylvie for the better part of a decade. Henri had always had a girlfriend, and other women besides, and the understanding was that Sylvie didn't like it but also that his philandering wasn't a marriage-breaker. She reserved the right to bitch about the money he spent on Lily (the current girlfriend) and about the Friday nights he always spent with her — Friday nights with the girlfriends, Saturday nights with the wives, a La Rue family tradition going back generations. But Sylvie was never leaving, not as long as Henri didn't rub her nose in it.

And, well, it worked the same when it came to her. And if she was occasionally fucking the fucking butcher, well, whatever. It was 1959, and he was a modern man in the modern world, and whatever. It was only Jack Quillette, only the goddamned butcher.

But this wasn't that. This wasn't Quillette making a delivery and then hanging around and making another delivery. This was different — the dress, the perfume, the diamond pendant.

Different. Not the fucking butcher.

Sylvie had always wanted to live on the top of the butte, and now they did. She had wanted it partly because it was a sign of status, to live on the top of Montmartre, but mostly because it was where Gérard lived — right out the front door and past the water tower, left at the first street, left again at Sacré Coeur.

Henri had counted the steps between his front door and Gérard's over the last few months. It was kind of a game to relax his mind. The way he had calculated it, it took about 220 paces to reach Gérard's house when Henri was in a good mood, when he had great news to tell the old man. It was closer to 250 steps, though, when his ass was dragging and he knew it was going to be a bad meeting.

This day, it was 252 steps.

Freddy had just told Henri about The Onyx. He came to the house to do it on Monday morning, early. Sylvie left them with their toast and coffee and took the newspaper out to the sun room — but she did manage to catch Henri's gaze on the way out, and to arch an eyebrow.

"Thursday, Friday, Saturday, Sunday — you wait until Monday to tell me," Henri said. He was yelling, and he was loud enough for Sylvie to hear, and he didn't care.

"I figured you should get to enjoy your New Year," Freddy said.

"You fucking idiot."

"We're completely clean," Freddy said. "It's not an emergency."

"The fuck it isn't."

"You read the story in the paper, right? You never saw the words 'La Rue' in the story at all — not in any of the papers. I checked them all, every day since. Nothing. Tiny got away clean. One of the stories talked about 'a tall gentleman,' but only one. And there have been no cops, not a hint, not a whisper. We have Tiny hidden away for a little while, but the rest of us aren't hard to find and the cops haven't been around."

"Where do you have him?"

"An apartment in the 11th."

"It better be a shithole. Fucking idiots."

"Look, why are you mad at us?" Freddy said. "I only shot the guy after he fired first — and he fired for no reason. Un-fucking-provoked. The Levines are the ones who crossed over the boundary line."

"Don't talk about boundary lines, you fucking—"

"Boss, I didn't break the rules."

"So you've said."

"But you know I'm right."

"I don't know shit right now," Henri said.

Freddy left, and Henri talked to Sylvie for exactly three minutes. That's how long it took for him to explain what had happened — about the casino, and the ambiguous business about the Rue La Fayette boundary, and about the dead Levine soldier and the attempted retaliation against Tiny. He was barely finished when she said what he had already concluded: "Unfortunately, you have to tell Gérard."

And so he finished dressing, and walked over, and counted the steps, all 252 of them. Gérard had been to Mass and had breakfast by the time he arrived, and was perched over an open ledger with Father Lemieux at his side. The old man's finger was tracing the figures, and then pointing and tapping in one spot.

"Henri," the priest said. He scooped up the ledger and left the room.

Henri took a deep breath and then just started spewing. If he managed to get it all out for Sylvie in three minutes, he took closer to 10 minutes with his uncle. Just going through the nuances of the peace deal he had brokered with David Levine, and the loophole through which Freddy had leapt when he set up the new casino, took half of the time.

About halfway through the recitation, Gérard leaned forward and held his head in his hands. Henri was afraid of what his uncle would say, so he elongated his explanation almost as a defense mechanism. He was starting to go through the bit about Rue La Fayette for a second time when the old man exploded.

"Enough," he shouted. Silent Moe, sitting in his customary spot — about 20 feet behind Gérard's left shoulder — seemed startled, and the newspaper behind which he was hiding ruffled.

"Enough," Gérard said a second time. The volume on this one was lower, replaced by a timbre best described as an imitation of a rabid dog.

His uncle then looked up, and there was a bit of color in his cheeks. Henri couldn't remember the last time he'd seen that.

"Are all of your men goddamned amateurs?" Gérard said.

"Freddy is my best weapons handler."

"No shit. But what's in his head?"

"I mean, he wasn't wrong about Rue La Fayette—"

"Don't even try to defend him to me," Gérard said. "You know he was wrong even if the letter of the law was right — and that's debatable."

"I don't think—"

"It's debatable at best."

"But the other guy fired first—"

"The mistake — the idiocy — was the casino. The rest, in many ways, couldn't be helped. But the casino toppled the first domino. Fucking fool."

"But—"

"Henri, will you fucking stop. It's indefensible. And it's no way to treat a partner."

"The Levines are a rival, not really a partner. The peace between us is like North and South Korea."

"With Rue La Fayette as the DMZ," Gérard said. "Which we violated. And now, well, now they really are rivals. Idiots."

Henri did not reply. Gérard had barely allowed him to complete a full sentence, and there was going to be no winning any element of the argument. Henri could see that. It was on days like this one that he felt the most demeaned. He ran the business, made the day-to-day decisions, assisted his brother's end of the operation when Martin made a mess that needed cleaning up, and allowed Gérard to sit in this living room with the Louis-the-somebody furniture and the painting by Van Gogh hanging on the wall.

"A minor work, but still," is how Gérard inevitably described it to visitors, and the false modesty always burned Henri. Days like this one were the worst, though. Days like this one, where he was the boss no longer, where he was the nephew in short pants and without a single hair on his balls.

The two avoided eye contact, which wasn't easy given that they were sitting directly across from each other in the fussy Louis-the-somebody chairs. Instead of meeting Gérard's eyes, Henri focused on his complexion. Almost as quickly as the color had entered his cheeks, it was receding. The color of his face again was gray, and the animation of just a few seconds earlier had been replaced by the overall sense of exhaustion. The silence was interrupted only by a cough, and then a second cough, and then Gérard leaning over and spitting into an empty espresso cup.

"Nothing else happens without my say-so — nothing," is what his uncle finally came up with. "Got it?"

Henri nodded.

"And make sure all of your numbskulls get it, too," Gérard said, and then he coughed again.

Since he had agreed to move into the house and stay there a few nights a week, Gérard had given Father Lemieux an office to work out of during the day — a small, bright room down the hall from the kitchen and next to the pantry. That was where he left the ledger before returning to the kitchen with two new jars of Gérard's favorite marmalade, one orange and one peach.

The marmalade was put up by the two sisters who did the cooking at the cardinal's rectory. They spent an entire day in August every year doing the cooking and then pouring their creation into small jars. When Gérard had told him what he ate for breakfast every day — coffee, toast, and marmalade — the priest had insisted that he try the nuns' creation. Gérard pronounced it the best he'd ever eaten, and Father Lemieux had supplied him with new jars on a regular basis for more than two years.

The fruit was so sweet, as it turned out, that Gérard had never been able to taste the arsenic. Of course, Alain Benneville had said, "The stuff is tasteless. You could put it in by the pound, and he would never know." But the doctor had told him just an eighth of a teaspoon would do what was required, and that was the amount that the priest had carefully stirred into each of the jars that he replaced about every month. He kept the supply of arsenic in his room at the rectory, a small tin that Benneville had gotten for him from a chemist. It was hidden at the bottom of the basket of his out-of-season civilian clothes that he kept in the back of the closet. He dreamed sometimes of a police raid, and of some gendarme pawing through the sweaters and wool slacks in summertime and finding the half-empty tin at the bottom and brandishing it to one of the detectives with a flourish and a "Voilà!" The dream was waking him regularly now, almost weekly. The most recent was two nights earlier, and it had been like a scene from a bad movie, with him sitting upright in his bed and blocking some imaginary punch from a cop with his raised arms, sitting up until he realized.

That day, with Henri out in the living room meeting with Gérard, Mrs. Lebreque — the cook who came in to make

Gérard's lunch and dinner every day — was peeling carrots at the kitchen table when Lemieux came in with the new jars. He always told her that the nuns would reuse the old ones when he took them away, but he tossed them into a trash can on the street instead. It made no sense — there wasn't enough arsenic in the near-empty jars to hurt anyone in the short run — but he still did it anyway.

———

There were two ways that a truck from the south would approach Les Halles — either from the quai along the right bank of the Seine or the one along the left bank. It depended mostly on the driver's preference as there was no way to predict the traffic. Besides, after midnight, there was little traffic on either quai. The bottleneck would come later.

If the truck came up the left side of the river, the crossing point over to the right was at Pont Neuf. If it came up the right side, the turnoff was on Rue du Pont Neuf. Either way, left bank or right bank, the truck ended up at the same place.

From Pont Neuf to Les Halles, it was only about a half-mile. Most of that was a straight shot on Rue du Pont Neuf — and, again, there was little or no traffic in those two minutes. It was after that, at the end, where the jams happened — right on Place Maurice Quentin, right on Rue Berger, left on Rue Baltard, left again on Allée Baltard. That led directly into the loading and unloading bays of Les Halles, where a worker would determine the cargo and point the driver to the proper stall — fruits and vegetables one way, meats another, fish another. Except, as the clock approached 2 a.m., the meat and fish for the day had pretty much already been delivered. They had been on ice for hours and were being picked over by the chefs (in a few cases) and purveyors (in most cases). It was a busy place at 2 a.m. — fish being flung about, and arguments about thumbs on scales gaining volume, and money changing hands. The whores were pretty much gone by then but the rest of the commerce was flourishing at 2 a.m. That also was when the fruits and vegetables were arriving, to be uncrated and stacked and readied for another round of chefs and purveyors who would show up, bleary-eyed, around dawn.

Michel had studied the place for two nights after he had beaten the information out of Frankie Brière in the garage in Montmartre, just to make sure he understood the logistics. He had positioned himself along the route, and watched the flow of traffic, and determined that the place to make his move was not on Rue Baltard, where the line of trucks began to form, but before that. At the spot where Place Maurice Quentin intersected Rue Berger, the truck would have to stop at the sign before making the right turn — and that was where Michel would act. The stop sign was one reason, and the ability to make a left turn at the intersection, away from the rest of the truck traffic, was the other.

He looked at his watch — 1:45. The truck with the tomato stenciled on the side would be there at any time.

Michel was alone, which he knew was idiotic — but he couldn't figure another way, not yet. If this was to be his personal business, not La Rue family business, he could not logically involve any of the people on his payroll. There were a couple whom he trusted, but still. It wasn't right to involve them because of the potential consequences — at least not at the initial stage. Maybe later, but not at the beginning. There was the thought of hiring a couple of men for the night, but Michel also rejected that notion. Anybody worth a shit was already working for somebody else, and this had to remain a secret.

So, it was only Michel and the silenced pistol in his jacket pocket. He was leaning against a stone wall at the corner where the stop sign was, leaning and drinking coffee out of a paper cup, leaning and clocking the trucks as they passed. They were driving by about one every four minutes at that point. The closest interval had been two minutes. If he had bad luck, the interval would be one minute. Extremely bad luck, 30 seconds — but even that would be enough time.

The big question: would the driver be alone or accompanied by a passenger? And would the passenger be armed? The trucks passing by were about 50-50 when it came to men riding shotgun, and there was no way to know. Given that the truck with the red tomato stenciled on its side was loaded with a crate of heroin hidden among the produce, a passenger made sense — and a passenger with a gun made the most sense. But there was a decent chance that the driver knew nothing about the heroin, that he thought he was just delivering his usual shit, and that the men doing the unloading were the only ones who knew. In that case, maybe the driver by himself was how it would go.

That Michel was praying for a solo driver went without saying. If the guy was alone, he might actually survive the incident. If there were two of them, well...

The corner was well lit, and that was a third reason why Michel had chosen it. As he watched the trucks drive by, he saw that he was able to read what was written on the sides of them from about 50 feet away. He wouldn't need to read this one, though. Just a stencil on the side. Just a red tomato. He figured he'd be able to make that out from 75 feet, easily.

And, as it turned out, he had figured correctly.

Michel saw the red tomato — it almost glowed beneath the street light, it seemed. The truck was driving at about 15 miles per hour, and as it slowed for the stop sign, he saw the man sitting next to the driver. Shit.

Michel undid the safety on the silenced pistol while it was still in his pocket. The truck stopped, and the brake lights flowed, and he stepped out of the shadows by the stone wall and followed the plan. It was simple enough. If the driver had been alone, Michel would count on the man's hands being on the steering wheel, accost him in relative safety, climb into the cab, bash in the driver's skull with the butt of the gun, and toss the guy out the driver's side door and onto Place Maurice Quentin. But if the driver had a companion, well…

The truck stopped. The passenger side window was open — maybe because the guy on that side was smoking, maybe for the fresh air to help them stay awake. Whatever.

Michel fired once, up into the cab, and hit the passenger in the forehead. Then he stepped up on the running board and fired a second time. The driver also was hit in the forehead, his shrieking silenced after maybe two seconds. The passenger went out his door, the driver out his door; splat, splat. Michel looked into his rear-view mirror and saw no headlights. He turned left, away from Les Halles, leaving the two bodies in Place Maurice Quentin. The garage he had acquired for the purpose of stashing the truck was way over in the 14th, and Michel crossed the Seine on the Pont des Arts. There was no one following him across the bridge, so it was easy enough to stop and toss the pistol over the side and into the water.

In recent weeks, Thursdays had become "lunch with the girls" day for Sylvie. After two in a row, well, that was enough of a pattern for Henri to begin to take action.

He was pretty good, he thought, at not tipping his hand — but Sylvie was his wife, after all, and wives knew all of the tells. He wasn't kidding himself there. So he sat in the living room and hid behind his newspaper, which was customary enough on a day when he wasn't in the office.

Sylvie was in and out of the bedroom — dressed only in her slip when she walked past him and into the kitchen to retrieve her purse. He smelled the perfume again, the Saturday night perfume. And while he thought of a dozen wisecracks that would maybe dent her cheerful exterior, or at least indicate to her that he was noticing the care with which she was preparing herself, he said nothing. That was the smart play. But then he thought about it, and wondered if his silence would be its own tell — that his outward blindness to her getting dolled up again on a Thursday afternoon would signal louder than anything to Sylvie that he knew what was going on. Shit. He debated all of this in the time it took her to walk across the living room — like, three seconds — and settled on silence. The only noise he made was when he turned the newspaper page.

Sylvie didn't close the bedroom door, and he could see her in front of the mirror when he lowered the newspaper a smidge. He could see her primping, and fussing with her hair, and then stepping into a dress that, again, was just a little too much for lunch with the girls. She zipped it up without needing his assistance, and without the hint of a struggle. Was she a little thinner now, too? And, all the while, she was whistling the same song that she had been whistling for weeks in little snatches: "Love Me Tender," the Elvis song.

When Sylvie got the zipper up, that was his cue.

"I'm out of here, honey."

"Home for dinner?"

"Yeah, just a couple hours in the office."

"Okay, then."

"Enjoy your lunch," Henri said, and then he was gone — right out the front door and two blocks straight ahead. That was how close they were to the Place du Tertre, where there were a half-dozen restaurants to choose from, all of them facing the square where the artists painted, and sold their work, and asked every female who walked by if they could sketch her portrait. Six, no seven restaurants on the square itself — with a dozen more within two blocks. Sylvie lived at the top of the butte now, and this would be where they would meet for lunch.

When he reached the square, the taxi rank was a few yards to the right. Henri went left, though, and walked up to an old black shitbox, and rapped on the driver's side window. The kid in the front seat, snoozing, nearly jumped out of the seat and hurriedly roused himself and opened the door.

"Mr. La Rue, I'm sorry…"

"No worries. I used to work nights, too."

The kid, who everyone called JJ, was one of Passy's bartenders at Trinity One. He handed Henri the keys, and Henri peeled off a bill from his roll and handed it over in return.

"No, no, Mr. La Rue — I can't accept this."

"JJ, you can accept and you will accept. There's no discussion. You're doing me a great favor."

"But I didn't even have time to clean—"

"No worries — like I said, I was your age once," Henri said. He looked over JJ's shoulder into the backseat and saw an empty coffee cup, an old newspaper, and what appeared to be a bra strap poking out from beneath the old newspaper. Yes, he had been that age once.

Henri settled into the seat, only his eyes and the top of his head showing above the dashboard. He could see the taxi rank just fine. It wasn't five minutes later when he saw Sylvie reach the square, turn right, and get into the first taxi in line. He was right, and he generally liked being right. Except, well…

Down the butte, down, down. Henri wasn't much on espionage or subtlety, but he was able to follow the taxi pretty easily through the midday traffic. Sometimes he was right behind it, but he wasn't worried — not until he saw Sylvie open up her compact, and look in the little mirror, and reapply a dab or two of powder on the nose and forehead. Even then, though, he knew she wasn't looking at anything in the mirror but her face.

Down, down, down the butte, and then into the 9th, and then a right turn heading to the 8th, and then Henri knew. Well, he didn't know the exact destination, just the area. Sylvie was heading toward the Champs-Élysées. Maybe it was lunch with the girls and then a little shopping — but, no. The dress, the perfume, the whistling — fuck, no.

Henri knew the area well. Lily's apartment was right on the Champs itself. It had been Marina's apartment before Henri decided to make a change. He had never really liked Marina all that much, except for how she filled out the Dior dresses that arrived on a monthly basis. Lily had been a clerk in a dress shop just down the street, and she had blown Henri in one of the dressing rooms while he was shopping for a birthday present for Sylvie, and Marina had become a little too fond of the white powder, and it was just time. It had been nearly two years, after all — or, as Timmy said when he heard, "Well past time to rotate the crops."

So, Lily's apartment was on the Champs — newly painted and furnished; she fucking loved the color lavender — and his brother Martin's place was on Avenue Montaigne, a 10-room duplex that looked like it was out of one of those design magazines. No, Montmartre wasn't good enough for Martin, not even the top of the butte. He always said it was because the legitimate end of his business — the wine and liquor importing part — required him to be in that part of town day and night, but it was bullshit. Avenue Montaigne was Martin's way of jabbing both his uncle and his older brother, his smarter brother, his from-the-neighborhood brother with his from-the-neighborhood wife. Martin and Marie were not Montmartre people, but Avenue Montaigne people, and fuck the butte, even the top of the butte.

There was now a single car between the shitbox and Sylvie's taxi. They were right on Champs-Élysées, passing Lily's apartment and then the turn onto Avenue Montaigne. Two blocks later, the taxi made a right and then coasted over to the curb about 300 feet down. Henri was able to park about 150 feet behind.

They were on Avenue Dutuit. The taxi stopped in front of a stately building — real money. If Henri had his bearings correct, he was pretty sure that the goddamned Petit Palace was in the building's backyard.

The door of the taxi opened, and Henri scrunched down in the driver's seat. He saw Sylvie's right leg, and the hem of her red dress — but, before it reached the pavement, a man was there and reaching into the taxi with his right hand. He must have been waiting at the front door.

As the man assisted his wife from the taxi, Henri did his best to imprint the details — not that it required any special effort. If anybody had been keeping track, they would have seen that Henri hadn't blinked since he pulled the car to the curb.

The man reaching into the taxi was a little younger than Henri and a little trimmer, despite the fact that Henri had been lunching on his customary Salad Niçoise, but without the egg, for several weeks. Younger, thinner, more hair, too — fuller and almost blond. After paying the fare, the man hugged Sylvie on the sidewalk — hugged, then kissed, then held her hand as they walked up the steps and into the house.

There was so much Henri didn't understand at that moment, didn't know. But as he sat there, slumped in the shitbox, peering over the dashboard, there was one certainty: Sylvie wasn't fucking the butcher anymore.

PART V

PINK BALLET

Guy arrived at the skank place about 4 p.m., having slept till 1. There had been a fight the night before, and he had to stay late to see to the damage: a broken table, a whisky stain on the wall from the shattered bottle, and the bit of blood on the corner of the rug. He didn't do the cleaning but he supervised it, hovering over his guys — especially the one working on the rug — with the admonition he'd heard his mother offer a hundred times: "Blot, don't rub, you stupid motherfucker." Well, he added the "you stupid motherfucker" part.

Meanwhile, the plumber was just getting done fixing the sink in the girls' bathroom. He got the key from the dry cleaner next door, as did all of the workmen Guy hired for maintenance and repairs and whatnot. They all came earlier in the day — the instructions were to be done by 4 — and Guy allowed them to have the run of the place while they worked. There was nothing worth stealing — nothing that wasn't locked in the office safe — except for the alcohol. And who was Guy to deny a man a quick one after he fitted a new washer into one of the taps?

It was Thursday, which was payday. The plumber was gone, and Guy was alone. He liked that first hour, alone. It allowed him a minute to get organized. Timmy had explained how he did things at Trinity One, and Guy followed the same script — except for the part about banging all of the girls before he hired them. Guy was very much from the you-don't-shit-where-you-eat school of whorehouse management. When he was so inclined, which was less often than he'd expected, he partook of one of Timmy's girls at Trinity One, on the house.

Friday was payday, so Thursday was when Guy filled the envelopes and made the notations in the ledger. It wasn't hard, not at all, in the same way that brushing your teeth wasn't hard. It was just a matter of getting into the routine and sticking to it. Maintenance check on Monday.

Ordering linens and other supplies on Tuesday. Recording the girls' medical checks on Wednesday; the doctor came right to the brothel to do them. Filling the pay envelopes and updating the ledger on Thursday. Then, fuck the weekend — there was no time for administrative work on the weekend, when about 70 percent of the weekly business took place.

The envelopes were filled, the ledger nearly done, when Sammy arrived at 5. He was Guy's second in command at the skank place, except that Guy almost never allowed him the latitude that Timmy permitted his top lieutenant. Timmy let his guy at Trinity One count the money at the end of the night because Timmy tended to disappear about 10 p.m., even on weekends. Guy just about always locked up himself — both brothels. The better place closed first, and the skank place on Boulevard de Clichy about an hour later. The drive between them was less than 10 minutes at that time of night.

Guy started his nights at the skank place, and then drove halfway up the butte to the nicer place around 8, and then returned to the skank place to lock up. He always beat Sammy to the office in the afternoon, and Sammy always brought him a coffee and the newspaper. Always *France-Soir*, the biggest tabloid in the city.

"What do you got?"

"Just linens and shit," Sammy said. One of his pre-opening tasks was making sure that there were enough bed sheets in each of the rooms. It was the girls' responsibility to change them between clients.

"How about the bar?"

"I restocked last night while you were supervising the, uh, the cleanup. The rug looks great in the light of day."

"But the wall looks like shit."

"Maybe half a shit."

"Maybe you take one more whack at it now — just five minutes. Then I'll decide if we need the painter."

"Or you could just rearrange the chairs a little and cover it that way."

"Excellent executive thinking — yeah, do that," Guy said, and Sammy was off with a smile on his face. Being a boss really wasn't very hard at all. You complimented the good workers, kicked the ass of the bad workers, and fired the ones who didn't fit neatly into either category because they were the sneaks who could really hurt you.

Guy finished the ledger and locked it in the safe with the envelopes and the rest of the cash. His father got his cut on Saturday afternoon. His father, who was such a skeptic. In his more honest moments, Guy admitted that he had been a bit of skeptic, too. He wasn't sure he would be able to manage and he was surprised how relatively easy it had been. He would never say that out loud, though — well, not in the presence of the old man, anyway. He'd said it to Gérard just recently, and Clarice had known all along how he tended to view himself as a fuck-up, mostly because he'd always been a fuck-up. He was smarter than he'd let on, but always a fuck-up in the end. But he'd never admit that to his father. Never to his father.

The coffee was cold when he sipped it, but that was fine. He turned over the newspaper, and the headline was a typical *France-Soir* screamer: "Dastardly Scandal!"

A thieving politician? A cheating celebrity husband? Those tended to be the *France-Soir* targets du jour. But then Guy read the smaller headline below the screamer: "The corruption of young girls at the 'Pink Ballet.'"

That was when Guy knocked over the cold coffee, yelled a curse, and mopped up the mess as best he could with the day-before newspaper.

And then, he read:

PARIS - A major scandal has erupted in the city following reports of a prostitution ring that is operating under the guise of a dance troupe. The troupe, known as the Pink Ballet, is said to be made up of young girls who are being exploited by wealthy and influential men.

According to sources close to the investigation, the prostitution ring has been in operation for several years and involves many of the most powerful men in France. The girls are allegedly procured by a network of individuals who work in the police department and in the entertainment industry and are then used for sexual purposes by the men involved in the ring.

The scandal is likely to send shockwaves through French society and lead to calls for greater accountability and transparency in the country's political and social systems. Many will likely ask how such a thing could happen in a country that prides itself on its commitment to human rights and social justice.

The first person arrested in the scandal is Jean Merlu, 34, who is employed as a driver by the police department of Paris. Merlu was arrested on charges of procurement and sexual abuse of minors.

The allegations against Merlu sketch out the outlines of the scandal. Underage girls were reportedly procured by a network of individuals, and the girls were then allegedly used for sexual purposes by wealthy and influential men in France. Unconfirmed reports suggest a prominent hairdresser, a large department store owner, and other men of significant means are involved, along with political figures who reach near the top levels of government.

The allegations of abuse took place at various locations throughout Paris, including nightclubs, hotels, and private residences. The exact site of the allegations against Merlu and the other men involved in the scandal is unclear, as the investigation into the case is ongoing.

According to the indictment against Merlu, he is accused of procuring young girls for three years. The youngest would have been 14 years old and the oldest 20 years old. Others suggested girls as young as eight years old were procured. The civil majority in France is 21 years old, and the sexual majority is 15 years old.

Merlu allegedly offered them to meet men who could, thanks to their status and professional relationships, promote their artistic careers. Supplied with alcohol and marijuana, they performed erotic shows for their audiences, followed by sexual congress. Persuaded to promote the careers of their daughters, some mothers were said to have consented.

More details are expected to emerge in the coming days and weeks. The French authorities have vowed to bring those responsible for the exploitation of the young girls to justice and to ensure that the victims receive the support and assistance they need.

The case will likely have a profound impact on French society and will raise serious questions about the abuse of power and the exploitation of vulnerable individuals. As the investigation continues, it is likely that more revelations will come to light, and the French public will be left to grapple with the terrible crimes that have been committed in the name of pleasure and power.

Guy read the story a second time and then a third time, just to be sure. The only name in the story was that of the police driver, Merlu. The name he was worried about was not even the subject of a hint. The truth was, he didn't know enough about him to know if there was a direct link with one of the people that had been hinted at, but that could wait. His name wasn't there, and that meant it wasn't an emergency. Not yet, anyway.

Guy left the office and yelled in to Sammy, "Got to check something up the butte." Out the door, he took his car to the big newsstand further up Boulevard de Clichy and bought every other newspaper that they had.

A seat on the floor of the Paris Bourse, on the famed parquet, was out of the question for Clarice — even with her windfall. There were only about 70 of them, and they were owned by the oldest and biggest brokers and had been forever. Most of the seats were passed down through the generations — and even the children and grandchildren who didn't want to get into the business could not bring themselves to walk away from all of that guaranteed loot. The last seat that had come open was five years earlier, in 1954. The price ended up being nine times the amount that Clarice had netted in the Zurich deal — and it had undoubtedly grown since then. It had likely grown by a lot.

So, the curb it would have to be.

"It's a term from New York, from Wall Street," Louis explained. It was after, when he was catching his breath and Clarice was washing her hands at the sink. That seemed to be when they had their best conversations, at least in Clarice's memory. After.

"But, curb?"

"That's what it was at the beginning on Wall Street — literally on the curb," Louis said. "The real brokers with the big clients were inside, on the floor of the exchange. The rest were outside on the street — the hustlers, the little guys who kind of worked in parallel with the big guys, buying and selling in smaller amounts for smaller traders who the real brokers wouldn't touch."

"Literally on the curb?"

"Yes, literally on the curb," Louis said. "But that was more than a hundred years ago. The curb is no longer — not on Wall Street, not on the bourse. The brokers have offices but they work the same way — joining together in small groups and bigger groups, doing whatever it takes to make markets and make the deals that the big assholes on the parquet couldn't be bothered with."

Louis put Clarice in touch with one of the brokers he knew from the curb, and she discovered that even with her money, it would be hard to open an office independently. The broker had an idea, though. Another broker — his office was just down the hall in the building that, depending on the wind, either did or didn't smell like Les Halles, which was about four blocks away — was 75 years old and had slowed considerably. Still, he had some capital and he had decades of connections with other brokers — and those connections were the grease in the gears. And old Marcel Lefebvre, well...

The broker walked her down to Lefebvre's office and made the introduction, after waking the old man from his post-prandial nap. He stayed and assisted in what began as a conversation — "You bring me a girl?" Lefebvre said, as his opener — and turned into a negotiation once the old man heard about Clarice's background. When it came to that background, she left out the part about her family's line of business — La Rue was a common enough name that most people didn't immediately make the connection.

They talked for two hours and came to a deal that was sealed not by a contract, but a handshake. In exchange for some office space and the ability to say she represented Lefebvre in dealings with other brokers, Clarice agreed to assist the old man in some of his dealings and to pay him 25 percent of her commissions. Other than that, their capital would remain separate. When she assisted Lefebvre with one of his deals, the accounting would go into his ledger. Her deals, her ledger.

If Lefebvre had insisted, Clarice would have gone to 50 percent or more. The commissions were what made most of the brokers on the parquet into wealthy men and most of the brokers on the curb into more-than-comfortable men — those tiny slivers of each transaction that they kept for themselves, tiny slivers multiplied by hundreds and thousands of transactions each year. But commissions were the last thing Clarice was worried about.

———————

Heroin scared a lot of the old mob bosses. Gérard was different that way — family was family to him, and money was money, and when a member of his family, a cousin like Michel, arrived with a pipeline into the heroin money, that was that. But in other families, other cities, heroin was like the electrified rail on the train tracks — forbidden and dangerous. Better to stick to the whores and the casinos and the loan sharking.

That was why Michel was dealing with Little Tommy Rheaume and not Big Tommy. Little Tommy was in his early 30s, like Michel. Little Tommy saw the profit potential in dealing heroin and he wasn't afraid. Big Tommy was afraid. Big Tommy apparently said things like, "Heroin robs people of their souls. I couldn't live with myself." This was the same Big Tommy who ran gambling and whores that broke men and destroyed families. Just don't take their souls. God fucking forbid.

The center of the Rheaume family territory was Pau, down in the southwest. It was a big area without a lot of people, and with few rules. The border with Spain was about 50 miles to the south, and as long as they didn't get too close to Bordeaux in the north, Little Tommy said, "nobody really gives much of a shit what we do."

"And the cops?"

"Half of them are bought and paid for, and the other half are blood relatives — or, at least, it seems like half sometimes," Little Tommy said.

They were having lunch in Limoges, about equidistant between their bases of operation. Little Tommy drove but Michel took the train, carrying everything he needed to bring in a briefcase.

They ate at a café that faced Place Jourdan, which was an easy walk from the station. There was some kind of war memorial at the far end, but where they sat, it was right near a statue of the man himself, Marshal Jourdan. He was drawing his sword and looking victorious. Because they never got statues made of them, Michel thought, you never saw what the losers looked like. Could you tell by their faces that they looked like losers?

The lunch was convivial enough, with Little Tommy drinking more than a man driving several hours should have been drinking. But, whatever. Michel asked him if he knew how to cut the product, and Little Tommy said he had a guy who did — and that was all. Michel really had little to offer, other than talk about the weather and whatnot. He had no real desire to join in when Little Tommy made fun of his father and his father's old ways, but he played along. If Little Tommy needed to believe that he wasn't a greedy bastard but a generational visionary instead, so be it. Michel was under no such illusions about himself.

After Michel paid the bill — "You next time," he said, snatching it from the table, beating Little Tommy's reach by a hair — the two of them traded briefcases beneath the table.

"Count it," Little Tommy said.

"I trust you."

"I insist."

With that, each of them peeked inside their case. Michel didn't count the money, but a glance and a riffle through the pile of bundled bank notes with his hand told him that it seemed right. Little Tommy's inspection was even quicker. Three bricks wrapped in heavy brown paper were easy enough to count.

E ver since the first story about the Pink Ballet, Guy found himself getting up an hour early every day, at about noon, and buying five newspapers at the stand around the corner from his apartment. He took them and his coffee, and he sat in the back of his regular place, Café Lydia, and read the stories on the Pink Ballet. He could have read the ones the café had threaded through the bamboo poles on the newspaper rack, but he wanted his own for some reason.

There were at least three stories per day, from *France-Soir*, to *Le Figaro*, and all the way up to *Le Monde*. The adjectives grew less frequent as Guy climbed the newspaper quality ladder, and the headlines grew smaller and quieter, but even *Le Monde* was covering the scandal. This story, this Pink Ballet, wasn't the typical fare left to *France-Soir*. This Pink Ballet wasn't just some movie actor caught in bed with his sister-in-law.

There were interviews with some of the girls.

"I was just trying to better myself. I had no idea..."

There were interviews with some of their mothers.

"If I had known, if I had had any hint of the evil, my God..."

And there were hints and innuendos about which men might be involved. No one was ever identified by name — not even the prominent hairdresser and the department store owner who had been mentioned in the very first story. But there were more whispers, blind whispers without attribution.

A police district commander.

A movie producer.

A movie director.

A best-selling author.

No names, though. The only other name mentioned was that of a woman, a Romanian ex-actress called Elisabeth Pinaj-eff. She was said to have helped procure the girls for the Pink

Ballet, working on behalf of her consort. *France-Soir* spent days making fun of the fact that some people believed Pinajeff was a countess, eventually quoting anonymously someone from the Romanian legation who said, "I'm a 50-year-old man, and I'm more of a countess than she is."

But who was Pinajeff's consort? He seemed to be the biggest fish of all. Yet, like everyone but the police driver Jean Merlu and the countess, he remained unnamed.

Three days before, this had been the story in *Le Figaro*, short and tart:

The police focus in the Pink Ballet scandal has shifted to a prominent government official who was said to have been a host of the drug-and-alcohol-fueled dance performances involving girls as young as 13, performances that were followed by group behavior of the most lascivious nature involving some of the wealthiest men of the Paris region.

Sources indicate that police are investigating the relationship between this high government official and Elisabeth Pinajeff, the former Romanian actress accused of helping to procure the young girls and organize the dance parties. Pinajeff was said to have been a close friend of the high government official. The Pink Ballets that she helped to organize were held at a hunting lodge in the Pavillon du Butard — located near Paris, in the forest of Fausses-Reposes. Other performances were said to have been held at a mansion in Seine-et-Oise.

One police source suggested that investigators were close to new indictments in the scandal that has rocked the nation.

And then, three days later, as he sat in the back of Café Lydia, Guy saw the story in the bottom right corner of the front page of *Le Monde*. It was below a story about an immigration bill that was stalled in the Senate and a discussion of the effects of the devaluation of the franc on livestock exports.

The headline was simple:

"Le Troquer Indicted"

The story was short:

André Le Troquer, former minister in several governments and president of the National Assembly until 1958, was indicted yesterday because of his involvement in what has come to be known as the Pink Ballet scandal.

Le Troquer is being charged with helping to organize the scandalous performances by underage girls and participating with other prominent politicians, police officials and industrialists in the lewd and lascivious activities that followed.

Le Troquer, 74, is said to have joined with his close friend, the Romanian ex-actress Elisabeth Pinajeff, in recruiting girls as young as 13 to the scandalous enterprise. Le Troquer is by far the most prominent name revealed by the investigation, which police say is ongoing and accelerating.

(Continued on Page 3)

The length and the positioning of the story on the page suggested to Guy that either the newspaper was embarrassed for Le Troquer, who had lost an arm in the first war, or that it had come by the information very late and just kind of shoehorned what it had into the newspaper right before deadline. Either way, well, whatever. That wasn't the part that made Guy feel like throwing up all over the stack of papers in the café.

No, the reason for that was the fourth paragraph, which was on Page 3 of the paper.

Guy took *Le Monde* with him to the skank place, and he was staring at that fourth paragraph when Sammy walked in on him with a cup of coffee for Guy and a copy of *France-Soir*. He looked at his boss and said, "They only have *Le Monde* at Trinity One. We aren't a *Le Monde* kind of place."

Guy ignored him, and Sammy left the office.

He stared at the bottom left corner of Page 3.

The fourth paragraph began, "In addition to Le Troquer,

sources say that investigators are interested in speaking to a group within the Ministry of the Interior whose connection to the case is not known at this time. It is understood that eight men from the ministry will receive subpoenas within days that will order their testimony in the ensuing weeks."

The story then went on to list eight names.

The fifth name was Serge Lemelin.

It jumped out of the paragraph as Guy stared at it. He could blur his eyes and still see the one name, Serge Lemelin. It taunted him. It almost winked at him. Fuck. Fuck. Fuck.

A million things were flying through his mind, but through that maelstrom, Guy was able to know exactly one thing for sure. He was going to have to tell his father.

PART VI

OLD HANDS

F our times a year, Gérard and Old Joe Levine had a meeting. They had been doing it for years, well before they began sharing business in the 10th arrondissement. Back then, the 10th — controlled by René Morel, an idiot — was the buffer between their territories. The La Rues controlled things in the 18th and the 9th arrondissements, from the top of the butte in Montmartre down to the Opéra. The Levines owned the business that was transacted in the 2nd and 3rd arrondissements. Back when Old Joe suggested the meetings, Gérard always wondered if he was thinking that René Morel, the idiot, would implode one day, and that a relationship would be meaningful at that point. And so it was.

Normally, they held their meetings at the Mazarine Library. Gérard had a longstanding relationship with Roger Cornette, the head librarian. They grew up together and went their different paths, but they still continued to participate in a two-man book club, working their way through the canon of different authors or time periods. They had been on 20th-century American novels for a while, but Gérard was getting sick of them. He hated William Faulkner, and *Absalom, Absalom!* was the last straw. At his next visit with Cornette, he was going to suggest maybe the Spaniards.

Old Joe Levine wasn't a reader, but the Mazarine was a beautiful building — the main reading room was breathtaking — and it was in the 6th, neutral territory. It was at those meetings that the two old heads anticipated problems and worked to head them off. When their families did clash after René Morel, the idiot, did implode, it was Gérard and Old Joe who worked out the peace between them and then convinced the people who actually did the work — Henri La Rue and David Levine, nephew and son — that peace was in everyone's best interest. Better yet, they both were convinced that they got the better of the deal.

This time, though, Gérard chose a different venue for the meeting — the Louvre. He arrived early and sat on the bench in front of a particular painting, "The Sabine women stopping the fight between the Romans and the Sabines." He had a point he wanted to make.

Gérard was a half-hour early, and Old Joe was 15 minutes early. They were like that, old-school early. Joe Levine was a few years older than Gérard, but the recent illness that slowed him pretty much brought them up to equal in Gérard's eyes. That is, they both looked like shit. Levine didn't say anything when they sat down, but Gérard could see him being scanned up and down. He could almost read the questions in Levine's eyes, but he ignored them.

"I really like this painting," Gérard said. "Well, let me put it another way. I don't know if I like it that much, or I just like that the bench is right in front of it. I don't know. And people just breeze by and hardly ever stop after seeing the *Mona Lisa*."

They both stared. Neither said anything, not for about a minute, until Old Joe said, "This is just us, right?"

"Of course, like always."

"Henri doesn't know?"

"My family, my business. And David?"

"No, just us."

They both went quiet again. They both knew the subject, and Gérard thought about starting. But he waited.

"The casino was a violation," Levine said, finally.

"Not technically," Gérard said. He went over the terms of the agreement that had been repeated to him by Henri. Levine acknowledged they were the same terms relayed to him by David.

"So, not technically a violation," Gérard said.

"So, our world will be one of technicalities now, will it?"

"Regardless, the response by your young man..."

"My dead young man."

"He pulled his weapon and fired the first shot."

Levine waved his hand. "A stupid kid," he said, "A stupid, drunk kid."

"You acknowledge that, but you still come after one our kids."

"I was unaware," Levine said, after a long pause.

"As I was unaware of the casino," Gérard said, after a long pause of his own. Then, they were quiet for a bit, and then Gérard pointed at the painting.

"So many of the others, they paint grand battles," Gérard said, waving indiscriminately back toward another gallery. "But this one, just look at it. Naked children in the midst of the fighting. Bare-breasted women, right in the middle of it all. Young men. Old ladies. Most seeming to try to break it up. Others, not so much. But it is a fight among families, touching everyone in the families."

Gérard stopped. After another long pause, Levine said, "I get your point." And then, he said, "God, I feel as tired as you look."

They sat for a while longer. In the end, they agreed that their lieutenants would have to speak again, and that this time, Henri would call David and seek the meeting, and David would pick the place.

And then, with the quickest of handshakes, they were done. Old Joe Levine got up first, and Gérard watched him walk back toward the crowd in front of the *Mona Lisa*. His driver met him there, and they kept walking. They didn't stop to crane their necks for a look at Da Vinci's lady along with the rest of the school kids and the yahoos. They never broke stride — although stride was pushing the reality. It was more like a shuffle.

At about the same time, Silent Moe joined Gérard on the bench, and they sat for a good half-hour. They gave Levine a chance to leave the museum. Gave him a chance to find his car. Created some time and space. Old men, old school.

***

H enri and Sylvie decided on sandwiches for lunch, and he walked up the street to pick up a couple of chicken tarragon baguettes, their current favorite. It was when he walked in the door that Sylvie told him about the phone message:

"Mr. Brown, 2 p.m."

Sylvie knew from prior experience that Mr. Brown was actually Inspector Chrétien, the most prominent cop on Henri's payroll, and she worried whenever he called. Henri normally did, too, because when Chrétien reached out, it was normally to warn him about some bit of police business that was in danger of taking a hunk out of his ass. It was Chrétien who had warned Henri about Guy's involvement months earlier in some bank robberies, something Sylvie remembered well.

"It's not Guy, you don't think?"

"No, no," Henri said. "No worries on this one. It's got to do with the Gare du Nord. Freddy's been approached by a new captain in that precinct, a new police captain with his hand out. I just asked Chrétien to look into the guy for me."

"Thank God," Sylvie said, and the two of them tucked into their sandwiches. Henri lied by reflex sometimes and managed it with significant skill. He had thought up the story about the Gare du Nord on the spot, in that second, and delivered it with just the right tone. Sylvie bought it, and there was no question of that. Henri, though, had to force himself to eat — and even with that, only finished a little more than half.

His customary meeting place with Chrétien was the little park on Rue Burq, which was on a little uphill street in Montmartre that pretty much led nowhere. There was a playground for kids, and six benches around a dirt square that was perfect for boules but which was perpetually unused. Usually, the only people in the park were young mothers pushing children on the swings. But at 2:30 on that day there was no one.

Henri usually arrived first, but not this time. Chrétien had removed his hat and was taking a bit of the winter sun.

Without a word, Henri reached into his breast pocket and removed an envelope. It was time for Chrétien's regular payment, anyway. The cop stuck it into his own breast pocket and simultaneously removed his small notebook, the one that all cops carry inside of a leather sleeve.

"You want the pages?"

"No, just read them to me."

"I mean, when I'm done."

"No, just read them," Henri said.

And that is what Chrétien did. Henri had given him the address on Avenue Dutuit and a general description — 40ish, medium height, blond-ish, and sent the inspector to find out what he could. He didn't tell the cop why, though.

"Name is Lucien Richard," the cop said, reading from the notes. "Address on Avenue Dutuit, as you said. From his driver's license, he is five foot ten and 165 pounds. Hair is listed as light brown. Eye color is listed as blue."

Chrétien flipped over the page.

"Profession on his tax registration form is, and I quote, dealer in modern and experimental art. The address of the gallery is on Rue Bayard. Maybe a 10-minute walk from his house."

"Experimental?"

"Don't know — maybe when they just splash the paint on the canvas like a kid."

"Maybe."

"But I know one thing — there's clearly a lot of fucking money in it. The guy's fucking loaded."

"How do you know?"

"You mean, besides the house where he lives and the street where his gallery is located?"

"Yeah, besides."

"I was able to do a very quick bank check on him, very hush-hush," Chrétien said. "I have a friend — no need for you to know more than that. It didn't take more than one question: What do you know about Lucien Richard?"

"And?"

"And, the answer was, 'Don't ask. He has so much money, I think God might strike me down for even inquiring.'"

Chrétien said he didn't have much more, but he flipped the page and remembered: "Oh, also a pillar of the church."

"Meaning what?"

"A member of his parish finance committee, and also serves as an usher on many Sundays."

Perfect. Just fucking perfect. As he watched Chrétien tear out the pages from the little notebook, hold them over the empty wire trash can, and set them alight, Henri knew that it was everything he had feared when he saw Mr. Lucien Richard reach into the taxi and help Sylvie onto the sidewalk in front of his house on Avenue Dutuit. Not the butcher. Really not the goddamned butcher.

———

Unlike the previous time, this meeting would be on David Levine's turf. He described a school on Rue des Hospital-ières Saint-Gervais, and Henri agreed. He wouldn't admit to Levine, not on the phone, that he had never heard of Rue des

Hospitalières Saint-Gervais, and that he had barely heard of the nearby cross street, Rue des Rosiers. It was not a part of Paris where Henri had spent a lot of time in his life, the Jewish part. Levine, of course, figured as much and delighted in what undoubtedly happened as soon as they hung up. That is, Henri was forced to pull out a map of the city and begin searching with his index finger.

Passy went on an exploratory mission after Henri indeed found the street on a map, and came back a few hours later.

"I don't like it," he said.

"Why not?"

"It's a wide-open fucking street. There are all kinds of windows, all kinds of vantage points. We couldn't—"

"He's not going to kill me," Henri said. "We're partners, remember. Well, kind of partners."

"I thought it was peaceful rivals, or some such shit."

"Peaceful rivals, then. But whatever you want to call it, he isn't there to kill me. I mean, think about it."

There was a bit of an open square in front of the school building, and Passy and Timmy positioned themselves in plain sight on one end of the perimeter, maybe three hundred feet from the school door. They arrived ahead of Henri, and they saw two guys who were undoubtedly Levine's men positioned on the other side of the square, about the same distance away.

Levine arrived first, five minutes early. Henri arrived exactly on time. Levine was staring at the school and Henri couldn't exactly read the emotion on his face — maybe wistfulness, maybe regret. It didn't appear to be joy.

"I went to school here," Levine said. "A lot of memories. My kids, they started here, too — you know, before. Everybody in the school was Jewish, I think. I don't know if it was the only public school in Paris that was closed on Saturdays, but it might have been."

You know, before. Henri got that much without an explanation. You know, before the Nazis came in 1940.

"The principal of the school, Migneret, he was a great man — he saved a lot of our families," Levine said. "Really stuck his neck out for us, for our kids. Mine, though, they were long gone. My wife and kids went to the country in that first summer — down south. I remember, as soon as Sedan fell, we made the plans. They all bitched, but they were gone before the Nazis reached the suburbs. The men, though, we stayed here. Business, you know. We avoided the roundups because, well, because of the bribes. You know it was the Paris police who did most of the roundups, right? The Germans gave the orders, I guess, but our own cops made the arrests and drove the wagons. Our own cops."

"I didn't know," Henri said. They stood for a second, and then David Levine began to walk, and Henri followed along.

"It's hard, when you think about it," David said. Henri wasn't sure what he was talking about, but he was pretty sure. Being able to buy your way out of death, when others couldn't, must have been a burden of its own. A unique burden. What did they call it — survivor's guilt?

"You do what you can to survive," Henri said. "It is the human response."

"It's hard, though. Buying off the local cops. Buying off the Nazis. Getting to live because of my money while so many others..."

They walked down to Rue des Rosiers and made a left. Levine began talking about the pletzl.

"Pretzel?"

"No, p-l-e-t-z-l," David said. "It's our word for 'neighborhood.' The pletzl, the neighborhood, it was ours. It was the comfort of family and friends. It was the shared experience of a lifetime. It was safe. Mostly, though, it was ours."

They walked into Goldenberg's restaurant, where David Levine had his own table in the back, a little separate from the rest but not completely isolated — not that it mattered, because the place was empty. There were some old photographs on the wall. He pointed at one.

"Gare de l'Est," he said. "My family arrived there. Almost all of the Jews arrived there. When we had our last negotiation, you and I, the money didn't matter so much. I was always going to get Gare de l'Est. Because of that."

He tapped the photograph on the wall. Levine ordered matzoh ball soup for both of them. When Henri raved about it, and about the size of the matzoh ball, Levine smiled. Midway through, they began to talk about what they needed to talk about.

"The casino broke the agreement," Levine said.

"It did not, not technically."

"So, so…"

"A loophole," Henri said.

"And if the loophole had been on the other foot, what would the La Rue family be saying about the Levine family? That you were in business with a bunch of chiseling Jews — am I right?"

Henri didn't answer for minute. Then, he said, "But the response from that kid of yours…"

"Which I knew nothing about, just as I imagine you knew nothing about the casino. I mean, come on. It won't bring in enough to pay for an old whore's knickers. But, regardless — it is my man who is dead."

"It is your man who pulled the gun…"

"At the casino that never should have…"

"And then you go after my man at The Onyx…"

"The place where you killed my…"

They talked in the same circles as they ate their soup. They talked until their arguments had been exhausted. They both knew that they had been instructed to end the thing by Gérard and Old Joe, respectively. Well, Henri knew that he had been instructed and assumed the same about David. The arguments were just a necessary part of the show.

The deal they came to was this: the Levines would buy the new casino from the La Rues; the La Rues would pay a small cash sum to the family of the dead kid; Rue La Fayette would become a much more formal boundary between the two families; and if the La Rues saw an opportunity in either the whorehouse or casino business in the future, it would have to be on their side of Rue La Fayette and it would only be permitted after a discussion and agreement with the Levines.

It was all hammered out, and the two of them were having a coffee at the end when four of Levine's men bustled into the restaurant along with Passy and Timmy. The place was still empty, between lunch and dinner, which was a good thing, seeing as how the four Levine guns were drawn — two jammed into the backs of Passy and Timmy, two pointed at Henri.

"What?" David said.

"They hit the casino."

"The new one? We just made a deal..."

"No, the old one on Rue du Terrage. Lou is dead. Mickey is hurt bad. They just came in blasting, three of them."

David stood up and nearly knocked over the table. He, too, reached for his gun and said to Henri, "You goddamned..."

Henri hadn't brought a gun. He never considered he would need it, and thought it might be a sign of bad faith. In an instant, he made eye contact with Timmy. The reply he received was a shrug.

"Just wait," Henri said.

"You goddamned..."

"David, stop — it wasn't us. It couldn't have been us. I

fucking swear to you, it wasn't us. Let me make a phone call. Look, just let me do that."

David thought for a second and yelled out, "Kippy! Phone!" Almost immediately, a waiter appeared from the kitchen with a telephone extension that he plugged into a wall socket behind David Levine's table.

Henri reached into his pocket.

"No gun, my phone book," he said, and everybody with a gun took a half-step back, tensing and then relaxing.

Freddy was the only person he could think to call. As he dialed the number, he prayed that the fucking hothead hadn't decided that he knew best.

"Freddy, what's going on?"

"Nothing, boss. Waiting on a shipment of German crystal at the station, and..."

"Listen, the casino's been hit."

"The new one?"

"No, the old one."

Henri heard nothing but silence.

"Freddy?"

"It wasn't us, boss."

"Are you—"

"I heard what you said, boss. I listen. It wasn't us. Christ, we're all here, sitting around, waiting for the train in two hours."

"You're absolutely sure?"

"A hundred percent," Freddy said. "I'm telling you, we're all here. It wasn't us."

Henri hung up.

"You got the gist?" he said.

David nodded. He had been listening pretty close to the receiver. He looked over at his men, and the guns were put away.

"I think you should go," David said. "I'm pretty sure we both have some thinking to do."

The 14th arrondissement, a nice enough place, was a waste when it came to the business of organized crime in Paris. Sleepy JoJo Tanguay ran it as befit his nickname. It was a tired place, with tired prospects and a tired boss. The most important fact about the 14th was not what was in it, but what wasn't: Gare Montparnasse. The big train station, which linked Paris to the south, was close, just across the street, but it was outside the 14th and in the 15th. The only potential economic engine for Tanguay, then, was a traffic light away — and the light always shone red.

A ton of the acreage of the 14th arrondissement was taken up by Montparnasse Cemetery, and another ton in the far corner by Parc Montsouris and the International City University and its various buildings that housed students from all over the world. The university was founded in the 1920s with the idea of promoting peace and harmony among nations, and Sleepy JoJo Tanguay's neighborhood was the perfect place for it. Peaceful. Harmonious. Comatose.

The bar, called Descartes' Horse, was on one of the side streets behind the university. It was a student joint and, at any given time, conversations in a half-dozen languages could be detected by someone who took a lap around the perimeter. By scientific calculation, 90 percent of the conversations featured this phrase: "Will you look at that ass? No, that one. The red. Yeah, her."

At the booth that was deepest into the darkest corner of Descartes' Horse, four men sat and drank from a pitcher of beer. They could pass for students, but none of them had the credentials for university. Two were 21, one was 22. Philip Tanguay was 23, the oldest. That gave him the most stature in the group — that, and the fact that he was Sleepy JoJo's grandson.

They were on the third pitcher but showed no signs of coming down. The adrenaline was still pumping almost two hours after the hit on the casino. It had not gone without incident — Philip fired twice and hit at least one guy, he knew — but the money in the safe had been worth the effort. The masks they were wearing — half-masks that covered their eyes, like the Lone Ranger — were enough of a disguise. More than enough. No one knew them over there in the 10th, and none of the four of them were very distinctive looking to start with. The whole thing was clean. Or, as Philip pronounced every few minutes, "Fucking immaculate."

Philip's parents died in a car accident when he was an infant. He was raised by his grandparents until his grandmother died when he was eight. After that, it was just him and Sleepy JoJo in the big house on Rue Jourdan — and the old man raised Philip as he ran his business, with the lightest of touches. The kid had a generous allowance from the time he was 16 and no real supervision. And if it took him until he was 23 to begin to develop some ambition, well, he was developing — not that Sleepy JoJo had any idea. The casino was his first foray, and he was sure that there would be more.

"Success builds on success" was the other thing he was muttering, when he wasn't saying "fucking immaculate."

The adrenaline was the thing he felt more than anything, though. He figured it would ebb eventually, and that he would sleep as deeply as he ever had, but there was no sign of it, not yet.

"Fuck this place," Philip said, after the fourth pitcher. At which point, they all stood up and — after elbowing each other about the one in the red, headed out to a dance club in the 5th, near the Sorbonne.

PART VII

SHAKING THINGS UP

Other than being Gérard's daily lunch companion, Henri figured that at this point, Silent Moe's main job was arranging the chairs when there was a meeting in the living room on Cité du Sacré-Coeur — the Louis-the-whatever chairs that seemed so fragile that Henri always sat down gingerly. He was placing the last one when Henri arrived, the first. They exchanged greetings, and then Silent Moe returned to his place, a chair about 20 feet away from the circle and behind Gérard's right shoulder. About 30 feet back on the left was the standing desk where Father Lemieux was examining one of Gérard's leather bound ledgers.

"So, how's—"

"The same," Lemieux said. "But a little agitated since your phone call last night. Not a bad thing, I don't think. It kind of wakes him up somehow."

"But?"

"Overall the same," the priest said. "No worse, no better. Just kind of steady, for better or worse."

Gérard and Michel arrived in the room at the same time. He had called them both, and Martin, and told them the story of what happened in Goldenberg's restaurant. Gérard set the meeting time with a second round of phone calls. He had not spoken to Old Joe Levine — it was too early for that. It was impossible to offer wise counsel without the first clue about what they were dealing with. He was sure that Levine knew that, too, which was why he hadn't placed a call, either.

The three of them sat down, and they all looked at the empty chair. Fucking Martin. Gérard looked at his wristwatch, and then at the grandfather clock across the room as if to validate what he already knew, and shook his head and started talking. They would begin without Martin.

"Are we all agreed that this should be considered an attack on us as much as it is an attack on the Levines?" Gérard said.

"As much as?" Henri said. "I'm not sure about that."

"You know what I mean," Gérard said. "We share the territory, for better or worse."

"But it was their casino. It was their men. We can't possibly be responsible for protecting them."

"Protecting, no. But put on their shoes for a second. Imagine it was our place that got hit. We wouldn't expect protection from the Levines, but I think we would expect sympathy and support."

"Whatever the fuck that means," Henri said.

"It means what it means," Gérard said. "We assist. We support. We try to help them find out who did it. We offer our help, and they accept it or they don't. But the thing is, it's tricky and we all know it's tricky. We're not exactly partners but we're not exactly rivals, either. It's complicated, but it's the arrangement we have chosen. It's a dance — and we have to fucking dance if it's going to work."

At that point, the door at the far end of the room opened and slammed shut, and Martin arrived, out of breath. Gérard looked at his watch and shook his head, and Henri looked at his watch and shook his head.

"Sorry, but it was important," Martin said.

"Well?" Gérard said.

Martin began speaking faster than he could organize his thoughts and faster than he could be understood. It came out as borderline gibberish — and while Henri had learned to deal with that particular trait of his younger brother, Gérard had no time for it.

"Will you fucking slow down," the old man said.

"It was a dance club — you know, where you sometimes have to scream to be heard."

"Yes, I was young once," Gérard said.

"Had to shout over the lutes and such back in your day?" Martin said.

Gérard stared down his nephew and said, "So?"

"Like I said, it's not as if he wiretapped the conversation with modern microphones," Martin said. "My kid was undoubtedly drunk and much more interested in pussy than anything, but he heard bits of the conversation, phrases. He said the guy was really screaming to be heard."

"Are you going to tell us?" Henri said. He hated this about Martin, the inability to recognize the important parts, the fixation on the surrounding embroidery.

"Yeah, yeah," Martin said. "So, he heard three phrases clearly within about 30 seconds. The first was, 'That casino was a piece of shit — wait till next time.' The second was, 'Let them keep thinking we're asleep.'"

Martin paused.

"And?" Henri said.

"And the third thing was a toast," Martin said. "To the fucking 14th."

What that all might mean was nebulous at best. The 14th — that was Sleepy JoJo Tanguay's territory. Henri couldn't remember the last time he'd seen the old man. The La Rues had never had any direct dealing with him — and, if he had to guess, the Levines probably hadn't had any direct dealings with them, either. There was half a city between their territories — and unless things had changed in the 14th, there wasn't really anything worth wanting within its boundaries.

"You sure about all this?" Gérard said.

"That's what my kid told me," Martin said. "He didn't even know about the casino, about what happened. It didn't dawn on him to tell me until this morning, when the rest of us were in the office talking about the casino. And that's what he said he heard."

Michel had yet to say anything. Being from Marseille, he had no institutional knowledge about Paris and its various crime families — not beyond the ones that were contiguous to the La Rue territories. He listened, and then he looked at Gérard and said, "The 14th?"

"Joseph Tanguay," he said. "Sleepy JoJo to you and me. About my age, give or take. Knew him a little during the war. You know, we pretty much funded the Resistance, and sometimes had a meeting or two with the other families. In the catacombs, more than once — they're in the 14th. Stacks of skeletons just lying there, doing nothing. Kind of a fitting for JoJo Tanguay. I don't know how he makes a living. So much — what do you call it — institutional real estate? Not much of a business base. Lots of apartments. It's really a shit area — I mean, nice enough to live in, I guess, but I don't know how he fucking eats."

Michel asked about Tanguay's organization. Gérard shrugged and looked to Henri, and Henri shrugged, too, and said something about remembering a son being killed in a car accident years earlier, but that was it. They went back and forth, the three of them, talking about what they knew and what they suspected — and it wasn't much. Henri asked Gérard if they should bring the Levines into the conversation.

"Not yet," Gérard said.

"But—" Henri said.

"Not yet," Gérard said. The tone was unmistakable, meaning that this particular line of conversation was over.

Through all of this, Martin was a spectator. They were ignoring him, talking past him, not even looking at him. He had brought the key piece of information to the table, and now he was being dismissed as they always dismissed him.

"Henri, you work your cops — find out anything you can," Gérard said. "We pay them good money for a reason, and this is the reason."

With that, they were done — except for Gérard's final announcement. All of them were booked on a trip to Lourdes for two days. Attendance was mandatory — Henri, Martin, Michel, and also their wives. Gérard used the same tone that he did about calling the Levines. There would be no discussion, other than Gérard's simple pronouncement: "Personal time. Family time."

As Henri stood up, happy again that the chair had not collapsed beneath him, he stole a look over his uncle's left shoulder at Father Lemieux, pen poised over the ledger. The priest was smiling.

"Do you think it means...?" Sylvie said.

"Yeah, I do," Henri said.

"Did you talk to the goddamned priest?"

"Didn't have a chance."

"But why the hell do I have to go?"

"It wasn't a request. It was a command. And Gérard is still in charge. And that's why you have to go."

"But—"

"No buts," Henri said. "If this is really happening — if he's that far gone, if he's looking for a miracle cure — then this is no time to be fooling around."

"But, for Christ's sake, wives?" Sylvie said.

The first thing Henri thought of was that his wife would be forced to miss a date with the man who wasn't the fucking butcher.

"Look — it's not my call," he said. "We need to play this by the book. The boss says go, we go. And if this is the end for the boss, we make sure that we are loyal and true and all of that bullshit. Because if we look like opportunists..."

"You still inherit the top spot. You can look like the goddamned devil and you would still take over. It's the rules. It's how Gérard got it when your father died. It's how you got into the second spot when your brother died. It's the rules."

His father and his brother, Big Jean and Little Jean, died during the same bullshit robbery. It was his father just fooling around, "keeping my hand in," and the result was a bullet in both of them, father and son. With that, the younger brothers took their places, Gérard at the top, Henri just below.

But Henri was well aware of something else.

"You've heard of the golden rule, right?" Henri said.

Sylvie shrugged.

"Well, there are a couple of ways to interpret it," he said. "And in the language of the La Rues, in the late 1950s, it might be argued that he who has the gold makes the rules."

"And that's you," she said.

"Well, not exactly."

Again, his wife shrugged.

"Heroin smuggling is bigger than you think," Henri said.

"Bigger than all you do?"

"Maybe a little. More than maybe. I'm pretty sure the heroin money is the biggest percentage now."

"That Corsican piece of shit, he wouldn't dare," Sylvie said. At her most emotional times, that was what she called Michel, "that Corsican piece of shit." Except, she was wrong. Henri's cousin was as French as they were. The heroin trade controlled by Corsicans in Marseille, and that was true enough — but Michel was French and he had just made the connections with the Corsicans because he grew up among them.

"He isn't, you know…"

"I don't care," she said. "Hitler wasn't a Bohemian corporal, but that's what Hindenburg always called him. Didn't matter. You get my point. He's a worm. And there's no way."

"But what if Martin sides with him?"

"He hates Michel — and he's your goddamned brother."

"Your point being?"

"Your brother would side with you."

"Unless he hated me, too," Henri said.

———

C larice settled in quickly to the empty office in Marcel Lefebvre's suite. He introduced her to some of the other curb brokers with whom he coordinated, and then he left her alone.

That she was good at analyzing markets became quickly apparent to all of her new associates, and they brought her in to assist with various trades every day. She worked with the La Rue capital and helped out whenever she saw a potential win, which was often. It became clear to her that many of her new broker pals didn't see the full potential of their positions sometimes — actually, often times. Most of them weren't trading with their own money, only that of their clients. Because of that, most of them were fixated on the number of transactions and not really the content of the transactions — because when it wasn't your money, all you were worried about was the two percent commission you received from every trade. More trades, more commissions — the result being a nice lifestyle but not a fabulous one. Clarice wanted fabulous. More than that, her deal with Uncle Gérard — 50 percent every three months — demanded fabulous. And the math was harsh because of the commission-sharing deal she had made with Lefebvre.

She knew this when she got into it, of course, but the truth was even more plain after a couple of weeks of staring at her ledger. Her trades were winners because she was good at trading, but they weren't winning enough. She figured, at her current rate, she could make maybe 20 percent in three months on the 5,000,000 francs that comprised the La Rue money — an incredible return on the portfolio. But 20 percent wasn't 50 percent, and incredible wasn't fabulous. The only way this was going to work was with bigger bets — bigger bets on sure things.

G uy had worked the thing in his head a dozen times, attempting to soften it somehow. To minimize his involvement. But the more he thought about it, well, fuck it. He figured, I'm not a child anymore — I'm a business associate. And this is business. And, well, fuck it.

So, after a dinner that included his mother, he asked his father to come out for a chat in the living room. Henri and Sylvie locked eyes for the briefest of seconds, and then let go.

"So?" Henri said. Guy had closed the door that led to the kitchen for emphasis.

"I have an issue," Guy said.

"Meaning, we have an issue?"

"Yes, we."

With that, Guy began to tell the tale. He began by asking if Henri had been following the story of the Pink Ballet in the papers, and Henri said, "Yeah, pretty much. And whatever I miss, your mother reads to me after dinner. You will not be shocked to learn that she can pretty much recite the stories from memory at this point. So, what's the issue?"

Guy paused, started to say something, then backtracked.

"Don't tell me..."

"No, no," Guy said. "I'm not involved. Well, not the way you're implying."

"I'm not implying anything."

"Imagining, then. I wasn't at any of them. I don't run with

that kind of crowd — you must know that. No little girls. Not me. No. Fuck no."

"Then, what?" Henri said.

"Well..."

Again, Guy couldn't quite find the way to tell his father. All of the rehearsals in his head had been forgotten.

"Fucking spit it out," Henri said.

"I might have supplied some of the girls — well, helped supply."

"What the hell does that mean?"

"Well, you know..."

"Just say the fucking words."

"All right, all right," Guy said. "I met a guy at Trinity One..."

"Taking advantage of the company discount, as it were."

"This is business, and you're going to start with that shit?"

"You're right," Henri said. It was something he almost never said, especially to his son.

"Anyway, this guy, he asked if I could maybe, you know, help him with a couple of young girls. I asked a couple of my girls if they had, you know, younger sisters who might — and they jumped at it. I mean, I really didn't even have to ask."

"But you did ask," Henri said. "And the girls who worked for you, they maybe might say that they felt it was the only way they could keep their own jobs, if they supplied their little sisters."

"It wasn't like that," Guy said.

"Says you. I mean, I believe you — but it's potentially your word against theirs. And you have no idea what your two whores might say if they were, you know, under pressure to save their own skins."

Guy was silent. He hadn't rehearsed this far.

"Tell me about your friend from Trinity One."

"He's on the staff of Le Troquer — but just a bureaucrat. Just a functionary. He's about one level removed from the guy who gets coffee. A small fish."

"And—" Henri said.

"I've spoken to him since the news broke in the papers," Guy said. "He swore to me that he's told no one, and that no one has asked. And I was feeling pretty good about that, until today, the story in *Le Monde*."

"Le What?"

"I can fucking read," Guy said. "I've been reading everything everywhere. And, here."

From his jacket pocket, he pulled out the story he had ripped from *Le Monde*. He pointed to the fourth paragraph of the story, near the bottom. It said, "In addition to Le Troquer, sources say that investigators are interested in speaking to a group within the Ministry of the Interior whose connection to the case is not known at this time. It is understood that eight men from the ministry will receive subpoenas within days that will order their testimony in the ensuing weeks. Among the names being considered for questioning are René LeBec, Jean Deveraux, François Beaumont, Antoine Moreau, Serge Lemelin, Pierre Dubois, Hugo Durand, and Jeffrey Richard."

"And?"

Guy pointed to the fifth name.

"Serge Lemelin — that's my boy," Guy said.

"Fuck, fuck, fuck. First mention, right?"

"First mention, for sure. That's why I came right over."

Henri thought for a minute.

"All right, all right," he said. "I wish you'd come a little earlier, so we could plan a little — but this is okay, I think. I'm sure you've figured that the danger here really isn't the law as much as it is the publicity."

"Are you sure?"

"The law? Fuck the law. It would be a slap on the wrist if it ever came to that — but I'm pretty sure we could fix it so that it never came to that. No, it's the publicity. I mean, people wouldn't be shocked that the La Rues deal in whores. I mean, come on? It's that the police would have to pretend to be shocked because we own so many of them. There would be the need to investigate. And when that kind of thing gets in the headlines, all the money in the world can't make it go away. And even if it would all end up being a slap on the wrist in the end, there's the time between now and then. We'd be frozen. We wouldn't be able to act. Our payoffs, our money — it would be no good. The whorehouses and casinos would be shut down — maybe even Trinity One. What we take out of Gare du Nord would stop. We'd still have the street money, I guess, but you can't feed your family on that. I know I can't. And if the investigation takes months, headlines for months..."

Henri paused, took a deep breath.

"We can't have that," he said.

"Meaning?"

"I think you know what I mean," Henri said. "But, look — we have the weekend to think. I'm pretty confident of that, just based on what the story said. We're going to fucking Lourdes with Gérard, so we'll talk Monday morning, first thing, here. Okay?"

"Lourdes?"

"Yeah."

"As in..."

"Yeah, miracles and shit," Henri said. "I don't know any more than that — but I think we can all add two and two. But, forget about that. Look — I'll leave you the number of the hotel. Between now and then, anything happens, you let me know. I think we'll be okay, but if I'm wrong, in any way, in even the smallest way, you let me know. Yes?"

"Yeah, yeah," Guy said.

I t was two days later when Henri had his last meeting before the trip to Lourdes. Well, second-to-last.

The first meeting was with Inspector Chrétien in the little park on Rue Burq. Henri had given him the instructions as soon as he had returned from the meeting at Gérard's house.

"The 14th? What the fuck do I know about the 14th?" Chrétien had said, when Henri told him what he needed.

"Then you'll fucking learn. Forty-eight hours."

"Jesus, Henri."

"Just think of the envelope next time if you bring me something decent."

"But—"

"No buts. Forty-eight hours."

It was just after dinner, and the night was chilly. Henri was buttoned up to his neck, sitting on a bench, when the cop arrived.

"About fucking time."

"Do you want to know what I found or not?"

Henri gestured for Chrétien to sit down, and then the cop began to recite from his little notebook.

"Sleepy JoJo is, as you might expect, not much of a boss these days," he said. "Not much going on. No growing or branching out, certainly. The organization is old. The captains are as old as the old man. The people below them are, they're like your age. One brothel. One casino. Minimal street money. No drugs. I talked to a guy in the 14th — friend of a friend, only a sergeant — and he said that they don't even bother keeping tabs very much. He said, the last time the Tanguays were really on their radar, it was about a dead whore. But the way it turned out, it was an old boyfriend who killed her, not the Tanguays."

"So, nothing?" Henri said.

Chrétien shrugged.

"You bring me shit?"

"Shit is all there is," the cop said. "Except for…"

"Except for what?"

"There's a grandson — Philip."

"And?"

"The guy told me that they brought him in a few months ago — selling cocaine in the toilet of a bar near the university. It was a setup — the kid he sold it to in the toilet was an undercover cop. But when they found out who it was, well, they let him go with a warning."

"And a stern talking to, I'm sure," Henri said.

"You're not the only one with envelopes," Chrétien said. He tapped his breast pocket. "But my guy said he was pretty sure they never even bothered to tell the old man."

Not nothing, then. Philip Tanguay, grandson. Not nothing.

Henri's last meeting was just a few minutes away from Rue Burq. It was at a little hotel on Place Émile Goudeau, either next door to or pretty near the Bateau Lavoir, which either was or wasn't the place where Picasso had a studio in the early 1900s. Was, wasn't, maybe, whatever — the hotel was where he always fucked Gina.

He had called ahead and she was waiting for him in the room, naked beneath the bedsheet. The relationship wasn't transactional, not exactly. Henri had gotten her out of the skank place, bought her a small work wardrobe, and installed her as a restaurant hostess with a friend up the butte on Place du Tertre. She was somewhere else now, a better restaurant, a job she had gotten on her own. In the time he had known her, Henri had offered her more for clothes and to get her out of her shithole apartment in the 10th, but she had always refused. She didn't want his money and didn't want to be his regular girlfriend, not that he had ever asked. She was pretty but not Friday-nights-with-the-boys pretty.

Other than the time he hid out in the shithole for a few days, Henri had never asked her for anything but sex, and Gina had never done anything but act like she enjoyed it. Except, it wasn't an act. She did enjoy it, as did he — in a way that was different than it was with Sylvie or his Friday night girlfriends. He loved Sylvie, after all, and they still did okay for a middle-aged couple. And as for Lily, the current girlfriend, the sex was like with the others, on an arc that bent over the course of about a year from "let's do it again" to "let's get it over with." With Gina, though, it was different — raw, primal, hard, fast, and exhausting. He was never not sweaty and spent when they were done — never until that night, when he couldn't even get started.

"It's okay," Gina said.

"The fuck it is," he said. The tone of her voice made it worse.

Because the thing was, they barely even talked when they were in bed, not until they were done and he was offering to take her out for a drink or a meal, an offer she never accepted. Even this short interaction was unnatural for them, off-kilter — Gina in tacit command, the one offering consolation.

He left her there where he found her, naked beneath the sheets. It was later that night at home, after a bottle of Bordeaux, that Henri was able to admit to himself what the problem was. And it wasn't the fucking butcher.

PART VIII

LOURDES

The train to Lourdes had some kind of equipment issue and was more than three hours late leaving Gare Montparnasse. What was supposed to be a dinner in Lourdes turned into a late lunch in the station instead. Seeing as how Gérard and Father Lemieux seemed to be the only ones who really wanted to go, Michel watched, as minutes turned to hours, the bad moods turn increasingly sour. Sylvie was muttering out of the side of her mouth and into Henri's ear, muttering non-stop. He knew, without hearing, that she was threatening to get in a taxi and return to Montmartre. Thank God they weren't in the same train compartment. As he looked around the lunch table, it seemed that only Romy stayed upbeat. The truth was, his wife also really wanted to go.

Michel had already made one phone call from a box on the platform, to offer a heads-up about the delay. When the train departure time seemed to be firmed up, he made another call. Yes, he said, the trip was still on. Yes, he said, he would be on time for the meeting the following night.

Michel felt the briefcase that was cradled between his legs as he stood in the phone box. He banged it off of one calf and then the other, as if he needed a constant reminder that it was there. Yes, he said, all good. Yes, he said, the same amount as last time in Limoges — same amount, same terms.

——

Sylvie and Marie had a relationship based upon a rivalry. Their husbands were brothers, nearly biblical rivals, and so were their wives. Most of the time, when they were alone together — which was almost never — they tried to one-up each other without insulting each other, which was quite a feat of verbal gymnastics. Apartments. Designer dresses. Hairdressers. Like that. For a time, the apartments had been the big thing —

but since Henri and Sylvie moved to their place on the top of the butte, the two of them were in agree-to-disagree mode. Marie liked Avenue Montaigne and the apartment out of a design magazine. Sylvie liked the top of the butte, the height of Montmartre, which had all of the luxury but also an artistic community and a more authentic feel to it — it was where she and the La Rues had grown up.

This day was different, though. They both were in a bubbling cauldron of hot water that was fed from an underground spring, submerged up to their shoulders. Their faces were slathered with some kind of mud potion, their hair wrapped in fluffy white towels, their eyes covered by cucumber slices. Maybe it was because they didn't have to make eye contact, or maybe it was for some other reason, but the conversation never once veered into the typical can-you-top-this.

Instead, it began with Marie saying, "Can you believe that fucking Romy?"

"I mean, honestly. What, is she bucking for sainthood or something?"

"Seriously."

"Like, has she suddenly forgotten what her husband does for a living?" Sylvie said.

Sylvie had drawn the line at actually accompanying Gérard and the rest of them to the grotto. The trip was bad enough. Lucien had been understanding when she broke the date — he was an usher at his parish, after all — but the whole thing had left her in a mood, and there was no way she was hoofing it up the hill and going to church and doing all the rest of that shit.

Gérard, it seemed, had figured as much. The hotel he had chosen, right at the gates of the whole Lourdes complex, had a spa building behind it. The Blessed Springs Hotel and Spa. As soon as Sylvie knew that, the girls' day was set — except for Romy, whose demure black church dress was paid for by the profits from heroin smuggling. She went with the men, leaving Marie and Sylvie to their hot water baths and their cucumber slices — and, after a time, a chilled bottle of rosé. And then a second bottle.

Sylvie was pouring for both of them when she said, "So, it's bad right now. Yes?"

"Yes," Marie said. There was no need for either of them to elaborate. This was their shorthand when it came to talking about their husbands and the state of their relationship. Sometimes it was okay — rarely great, but okay. Many more times, it was somewhere between "bad" and "I'm scared." Because, on the one hand, it wasn't as if either of them would hurt the other — not physically, anyway. But there were plenty of other injuries that both Henri and Martin could inflict on the other using tactics honed over the decades.

Marie took a long sip and said, "It's just harder as they get older. You know what I mean? It's just harder for Martin to deal with, you know, with the..."

"Dismissiveness," Sylvie said, and Marie nodded and took another drink. Dismissiveness. Henri did it to Sylvie, too — not as much with Martin, but still. She was a better partner to Henri than his younger brother — smarter to begin with, less inclined to the hair-brained scheme, a calming force more than anything, clinical in her dissection of a situation. Martin was none of those things. Martin was just stupid, Sylvie thought — but he was loyal, and they were brothers, and she had seen the way Henri cut Martin out of things sometimes with just a glance.

"Who knows?" Sylvie said. "Maybe the trip up to the baths will help them. I don't know how the fuck it's going to help Gérard."

At which point, they began to gossip about the declining health of the old man. Left unsaid, as they finished the second bottle and then returned the cucumber slices to their eyes, was what would happen after Gérard died.

Father Lemieux waited in the lobby. He was there a half-hour before the agreed-upon meeting time, reading a newspaper without any of the words registering, sipping a coffee but not tasting it. He didn't know why he was nervous but he was.

The plan had worked perfectly. His approach to Gérard had come on a particularly difficult morning the previous week, a hack-up-a-lung morning. It had exhausted the old man, the coughing fit, and he was slumped in his chair in the living room, the one where he could see the Van Gogh hanging on the wall. What did he always say when he pointed out the painting? A minor work, but still.

When the coughing got like that, he knew it was time. He was going to have to stop the arsenic, or Gérard would die. This was it. And so, while he was slumped in the chair, regaining his breath, Lemieux broached the subject.

Gérard's initial reaction was to thunder, "I'm not fucking dying."

"Nobody said you were."

"Then, what's the point?"

"You are a man of faith. I think your faith is greater than mine sometimes. You still make that walk to Sacré Coeur every morning, even today. You know the power of the place for the faithful."

"I'm not dying."

"I didn't say you were," Lemieux said. "But you have been ill for a long time — many months. And if you won't see a doctor..."

"I don't need one of those charlatans—"

"If you won't see a doctor, well, the waters, the power of the waters, it has been documented."

"But—"

"What could be the harm? A man of faith making a spiritual pilgrimage — even if you were completely healthy, you know there would be a benefit. So, let's just do it. I'll take you and Maurice."

"If I go, we all go," Gérard said. "Henri, Martin, Michel, the wives — we all go."

This was a complication that Father Lemieux had not anticipated, the whole La Rue caravan thing, but what was the harm? It wasn't a complication at all.

And there, sitting in the lobby, they arrived one by one from their rooms. Gérard was last, accompanied by Maurice, whom the brothers called Silent Moe. Lemieux and he had developed a bit of telepathic shorthand over the months — just a glance revealed the old man's condition. This morning, Silent Moe was frowning. It had been a bad night.

"We can get a wheelchair," Lemieux said.

"No wheelchair," Gérard said.

"It's close to a half-mile, I think."

"No wheelchair."

Henri imagined Lourdes was kind of like the American Disneyland, but for Catholics. He couldn't say that out loud, though. But as they walked up toward the church with the three spires — statues and murals framing the entrance, gold leaf accents shining in the sunlight — it was all he could think. There were hundreds of people walking along in the same direction, and it wasn't even summer. The summer crowds at Lourdes were legendary. There were restaurants — they had passed a few near the entrance — that probably made a year's worth of money in three months.

"A minute," Silent Moe said. Yes, said. They all stopped, and he went over to one of the dozen or so spigots from which you could fill bottles with the local water. There were people filling gallon jugs, but Moe had only a handful of tiny bottles, the kind that usually had eye droppers in them. The wait to get to a free spigot took longer than it did to fill the bottles.

"For my wife and her sister," Silent Moe said. Yes, said.

Once they reached the church, Father Lemieux escorted Gérard and Silent Moe up to a reserved area near the front. With a quick gesture, he pointed the rest of them to any available space in the back — Michel and Romy in one row, Henri and Martin a few rows behind them. From their spot, the brothers could watch their cousin and his wife. The two of them were on their knees and bowed over besides, Romy hidden beneath her black mantilla.

"Who woke up and named him Pope?" Martin said.

"Which him?"

"Lemieux."

"Just because he could reserve a couple of seats, I mean, big deal. If he was the Pope, he could have gotten us up there, too."

"Closer to God."

"God forbid," Henri said.

The church had uncomfortable wooden kneelers — but if Henri and Martin had sat down, they would be the only ones in the church who weren't kneeling. To distract himself from the discomfort, Henri began looking around. On the side of the church there were the customary confessionals — but these were different than he had ever seen. The booths were open from the back. The person confessing his sins kneeled and faced the wall on either side of the box where the priest sat.

"Look at that," Henri said, with a flick of his nose in the direction of the confessionals.

"Where are the curtains?" Martin said.

"Would you ever?"

"No curtain? No fucking chance," Martin said.

The service wasn't a full Mass, just a series of prayers that took about 15 minutes. After that, the next stop was the grotto. Lemieux took Gérard and Silent Moe and Michel and Romy up front. Henri and Martin sat in the rows of benches farther away.

"Is that it? I mean, really? Is that fucking it?" Martin said.

From where they sat, the statue of the Virgin Mary — placed in the spot where the girl saw her — seemed tiny. It was tucked into a spot in the massive stone wall carved by nature, ivy growing around the opening where it stood. Some of the people near the front got up and prayed closer to it, and eventually, they saw Gérard and the others do just that.

"Will you look at them?" Martin said.

"Which them?"

"Michel and Romy. When's the canonization?"

Henri snorted a laugh, and it was loud enough to draw a silent reprimand from the old lady sitting to his left. Seeing the stern look on her face, Henri snorted again. He couldn't help it.

Next was the main attraction. Henri had half an idea what it entailed, but Martin was clueless. When the attendant explained the procedure to them, Martin said, "No fucking way."

"You'll watch your mouth and you'll do it because I asked you to do it," Gérard said. Then he looked at the attendant and said, "My apologies."

Lemieux went with Gérard into one cubicle, along with their two attendants. Henri, Martin and Michel each went into separate cubicles with their own pair of attendants. Romy was taken over to the women's side.

Henri had been in small private cubicles before, but never with two men who took his clothes as he undressed and then gave him a threadbare blue cloth robe.

The cubicles were formed by curtains on three sides. The

fourth side, straight ahead, was the bath that you stepped down into. There was a bluish kind of stone on the back wall that Henri couldn't identify — it was a color he couldn't ever remember seeing.

The men actually insisted on helping Henri to undress — undoing the buttons on his shirt, supporting him as he stepped out of his trousers and then his underpants. They said the disrobing was as much a part of the ritual as the bath, the humbling yourself, opening yourself up to God's mercy.

Then, naked and supported by the attendants at the elbows, you stepped down into the bath after first praying for your intentions and then blessing yourself. It was the blessing that was the signal for the men to take you by the arms and down the steps. In the water, they instructed you to wash your hands, then splash some on your face to wash it, then to take a handful of the water and drink it. Then, back up the steps to drip-dry for a few seconds, and then back into your clothes and out.

The whole thing didn't take 10 minutes. When they got done, Martin said, "I swear that one of mine was checking me out down there."

"Disappointed, was he?" Henri said.

"You know very well, brother, which of us is the family leader in that category."

"A lot can change since high school."

"You didn't see the eyes of my robe-carrier widen," Martin said. "Nothing's fucking changed, brother. Nothing's fucking changed."

It was only when they were leaving that Henri saw a familiar face and followed him on the slow walk back to the town. Gérard seemed exhilarated, yammering on non-stop to Lemieux and the others while Henri hung behind and tried to focus. It had actually taken him a second to recognize the man — one of those out-of-context sightings that left him with that I-know-that-face feeling. Then it hit him. Could it really be?

The man, about Henri's age but a little more gone to seed, was pushing a woman in a wheelchair. When they reached the Blessed Springs Hotel and Spa, Henri allowed the others to go inside and said he was going to buy a newspaper. Slowly, he followed the man and the wheelchair another two blocks until they reached their hotel, the Laurel. It wasn't nearly as nice as the Blessed Springs.

PART IX

THE SORROWFUL MYSTERIES

Henri picked at his food and barely participated in the conversation. It was a big dinner for everyone on the trip, and Gérard was borderline ebullient as he presided, telling the old stories, drawing the old laughs in the familiar places — especially from Martin and Father Lemieux. Michel seemed a bit preoccupied, too — but that thought was in and out of Henri's head in a nanosecond.

Ronny Leroy. Fucking Ronny Leroy.

It had been nearly 15 years. Late 1943 or early 1944 — Henri wasn't exactly sure. The Nazis were still in Paris, though. Of that, Henri was certain.

Ronny Leroy. They were in their early thirties when it happened, but Henri and Little Jean and Martin and Passy and Gus and the others had known Ronny since they were kids. They went all through school together — and if Ronny wasn't in their crowd, he wasn't one of the kids they picked on, either. Sometimes, back in school, he was with them when the group got big enough, other times just beyond their periphery — but in neither case did anyone give Ronny Leroy much of a thought. At least, Henri didn't.

Early 1944, probably. It was cold out — heavy coats and watch caps. They were older then, married — well, not Martin, but the rest of them were — and working in the Resistance. It was a La Rue family sore point. The elders — Henri's father, Big Jean, and Uncle Gérard — thought the family obligation should begin and end with funding for the Resistance. The next generation — Little Jean, Henri and Martin, along with their friends — thought the Resistance obligation was more than financial, that it involved actual operations. They fought about it a lot, especially Big Jean and Little Jean, father and eldest son. And, in the end, the older generation could do nothing to stop the younger.

Early 1944, then. The bright young Nazi soldiers who arrived in Paris in the summer of 1940, the ones who tried to win over the French children with sweets and smiles, were long gone to the eastern front. Old, worn, gray men were their replacements — old, worn, gray and scared. They were easy pickings on the one hand but quick-triggers on the other. They weren't trying to win over anybody, just hoping to survive.

The operation was simple enough. Little Jean, Henri, Gus and Mikey Leblanc. Little Jean and Henri would place the bomb in the back of the truck that was parked outside the little hotel on Rue Lepic, the one that the Germans had commandeered. The Germans used the truck to transport soldiers to and from the daily assignments in their sector, guarding this and that. Gus had followed the truck one day on his bicycle, and then another, and then another, and noticed a predictable routine. First, the truck went to the German petrol depot on Boulevards des Maréchaux to fill up. Then it delivered the men to their posts. The trip to the depot took 14 minutes once and 16 minutes twice. The time spent in the depot was eight minutes once and nine minutes twice.

Gus told them all of this around a table at The Blue, a bar on Rue Caulaincourt that kept a stash in the back for the La Rues and their Resistance friends, a stash that didn't require ration coupons. The owner, Old Rideau (no first name), worked days, and days were when Little Jean and Henri and the rest did most of their planning and drinking. But this was at night, and the bartender was none other than Ronny Leroy. They hadn't seen him in several years, and they did the polite catch-up with him — not married, still living with his mother, blah blah — and that was pretty much it. They plotted their next move, and Ronny brought refills every few minutes, and that was it. He was as he'd always been — on the periphery but not closer. Again, Henri never gave him another thought.

"Hey, are you awake there?" It was Sylvie, dragging him back across the decades, back into the present, to a restaurant table in Lourdes.

"Sorry, just daydreaming."

"The old man looks pretty good — at least, better than he has."

"Miracles do happen."

"Miracles, my ass," Sylvie said. They both turned toward the head of the table as Gérard told a story that they all had heard a dozen times — all except Father Lemieux, probably. It involved a group of soldiers from Gérard's unit in the first war and a wine cellar up near Lille. It also involved a girl, except Gérard was leaving out that part, it seemed, to protect the priest's sensibilities.

After a few seconds, Henri drifted back easily, almost insistently. Early 1944, then. Coats and watch caps. They had finished planting the bomb in the pre-dawn. Rue Lepic was silent, and Little Jean and Henri were making their way back toward the others — perched behind parked cars — when the shooting started. How the two La Rue brothers were not hit still astounded Henri because they were in the middle of the empty street for about 10 seconds, and there were what seemed like a half-dozen rifles firing at them. The La Rues survived, as did Gus, but Mikey Leblanc took a bullet in the forehead and died instantly. Mikey Leblanc, father of two.

They all scattered, as was the plan if something bad happened, and met the next afternoon at The Blue. It was there that Gus, who understood enough German to be dangerous, said he heard one of the rifles shout, "Four of them, just like he said."

But who was *he*?

It took them a few days before they decided that it must have been Ronny Leroy, who heard enough as he was refilling the drinks. It took them a few days more to learn where he lived, a house at 43 Rue Petrelle. And it took another two days to hear about the Nazi captain who paid afternoon visits to 43 Rue Petrelle, where Mrs. Leroy was doing the entertaining.

When they went there to get their revenge, they found the house empty. Well, the furniture was there but the clothing was gone. Somebody had tipped them off. And if Henri thought less and less about Ronny Leroy over the years, he never forgot him.

And now, nearly 15 years later, he told Sylvie that he was going to get some air after dinner. He walked about two blocks and sat on a bench that was conveniently located across the street from the Laurel Hotel. It wasn't 15 minutes before he saw the light flick on in one of the second-floor windows. Through the lace curtains, he could make out a man helping the woman out of the wheelchair, and getting her into a night dress, and putting her to bed, and dousing the light. And then, two minutes after that, fucking Ronny Leroy came out of the main entrance of the Laurel Hotel and turned right. A block after that, he walked through a nondescript door with a sign above it that said "BAR."

Henri sat on the bench and waited. After 20 minutes, he got up and crossed the street and turned to the right.

Martin went out for some air after dinner, too. And if Lourdes was a town where the shrine was the main economic driver, and where everything seemed to be named after some-or-other saint, it was still a tourist town. And however holy the water they used to wash themselves during the day, the male tourists were still, well, male.

"There is one, right?" Martin said. He was talking to the bellhop in the hotel lobby.

"Three, actually," the kid said. He might have been 17, and he recommended a place on Avenue Helios, a block behind the train station.

"Tell them Joe sent you, please," the kid said.

"And what does Joe get out of it?"

Blushing, the bellhop said, "You're the fifth this month. Five for a free blowjob."

The place on Avenue Helios was fine, the cockroaches manageable, the sex both mindless and meaningless. It was the metaphor for his life, and he knew it. Mindless and meaningless.

The money was fine — running the liquor distribution end of the family business was a cash cow, and almost effortless besides. There was the occasional café owner who balked at a price increase, but Martin had people who took care of that for him. He only heard about the beatings after they had been delivered. And as for the legitimate part of the business, the wine and liquor importing part, that was all swell lunches and drinks at the Georges V, and gallery openings, and schmoozing in evening clothes, often with Marie in tow. She loved the life, that part of it. He should have but couldn't.

It was Henri. It was always Henri. Michel was a smug prick, but Martin could deal with that. It was the disdain from his brother that ate at him. He would be a better husband, a better businessman, a happier person if Henri would just treat him as something other than a nonentity. Like the other day — he had brought the news of the kid from the 14th, and Henri had taken the information and proceeded to ignore him. From Gérard, the treatment was almost tolerable. But Henri? His brother? The second brother who was only in the position he was in because of Little Jean's death? The accidental prince? That fucking brother?

It was where his mind tended to go, and way too often. Thus, the search for distractions. Mindless. Meaningless. One foot in front of the other. One hooker in front of the last.

After he was done, Martin was washing himself at the sink in the house on Avenue Helios, and it was where his mind wandered again, to the accidental prince.

But then he laughed out loud, and the whore said, "What?"

"Am I rinsing my balls in holy water?" Martin said.

"I guess it's as holy as any," she said.

Michel, too, went for some air after dinner. And if Romy noticed that he took the briefcase with him, she didn't say anything. The day had excited her and exhausted her, and she was half asleep with the Bible propped on a pillow in her lap when he kissed her on the forehead. Her eyes were closed, and her reply was nothing more than a small smile.

The café was down near the train station, a longer walk than he remembered. The taxi had taken them a different way, and it had been daylight, and Michel didn't recognize anything as he walked in the dark. Still, the directions from the hotel front desk were good, and The Saints' Rest was where the clerk said it would be.

On the telephone, when they were delayed at Gare Montparnasse, Little Tommy Rheaume had said the meeting would be in a small room at the back of the café — door in the far right corner. Four of the tables — four of maybe a dozen — were in use. Michel walked directly to the door in the far right corner without making eye contact with anybody.

When he opened it, there was no Little Tommy. Just two men he didn't recognize, one older, one younger.

"Oh, excuse me."

"Michel La Rue? Please, please, come in."

Michel hesitated.

"Michel, please — may I call you Michel? Please, please. Have a drink."

It was the older man. He was the one doing the talking. He pointed to the bottle on the table and to one of the two empty chairs. Michel didn't move. He was doing the quickest of calculations in his head. That Little Tommy was absent meant exactly what for Michel's long-term health? Maybe it meant nothing. Maybe Little Tommy was just late. The problem was that this was a private side deal. No one in Michel's family knew, and no one in Little Tommy's family knew.

The thing to do was to turn on his heel and walk through the café and pray that the taxi that had been idling in front was still there. Michel knew that was the play, knew it in a second. But then he felt the presence of two men behind him. They must have come from one of the other tables. With that, the only calculation that mattered was four against one.

"Good, good," the old man said. "But, before you sit..."

The men behind him each grabbed an arm. The one on the right took the briefcase. The one on the left reached under Michel's jacket and removed the pistol from the holster beneath his armpit.

"Drink, drink," the old man said, and Michel drank. The silence that followed was uncomfortable, but there was nothing for Michel to say. This was not his show. It was Big Tommy Rheaume's show. At least, that's who he assumed the old man was, the old man who poured, and drank, and poured again.

"My son," he said. Then another sip.

"My son, your partnership, a mistake," Big Tommy said. "More than a mistake — an abomination. You know what that, that brown poison does, yet you sell it anyway. You know how it robs a man of his humanity, yet you don't care as long as there is a fat profit margin. An abomination, yes."

He spoke like a cleric, Michel thought. He sounded like the back-room version of the priest who had preached during the day from the pulpit of the big church in the shrine. He had never been in the presence of such a gangster. In his world, decisions were business decisions in the end - profit and loss, risk and reward. Those were the elements that were weighed, and morality had no place at the table. Big Tommy was so different. A man's humanity? How much does that weigh?

"Little Tommy will never make the same mistake again," Big Tommy said. "I am certain of that. When he comes back, he will be a changed person. There is no doubt about that."

What he did to his son, or had done to him, was not explained. The question of where they sent Little Tommy, and in what condition, would be answered only by Michel's imagination — which was revving at an uncomfortable speed at that point. Redlining, in truth.

"You, though, Mr. Michel La Rue, I do not know you like I know my son," the old man said. "I do not know you at all — not in reality and not by reputation. I only know your actions. From what Little Tommy said — you know, after we found out — you were as disloyal to your family as he was to his. But from what Little Tommy said, yours is a family without morals. Yours is a family that recognizes the effects of that brown poison but that sanctions its sale regardless. You, you La Rues, you rob men of their souls and you line your pockets without regret."

Big Tommy poured himself a sip more and downed it in one.

"Without regret," he said.

And then he was on his feet, and then the other three were on their feet. Two made a show of removing their pistols, making sure Michel saw them, and then replacing them in their side jacket pockets. They walked behind Michel as Big Tommy and the other guy led the way out of the back room, and then out of The Saints' Rest, and onto the sidewalk. The train station was across the street, and that was the direction in which the five of them walked.

Martin didn't feel like walking back to the hotel, and there had been a couple of taxis in a rank at the train station, and that was where he was headed from the brothel on Avenue Helios when he saw what he saw: Michel, surrounded by four men as if he were in the middle of a human cage, all of them entering a side door of the station.

He followed as closely as he dared, cracked the side door, and saw Michel and the human cage entering through an inner door that was down a hallway lit by a single overhead bulb. Martin counted to five and then crept down the dimly lit hallway. The door through which Michel had been escorted was still open a crack. Martin couldn't see much but he could see enough: Michel on a chair, another single bulb lit above his head, the four men — their backs all facing the door — taking turns kicking his cousin and then pistol-whipping him. And then one of them — he sounded old — opened the briefcase and waved it at Michel and said, "The brown poison. Where do you get it? Where?"

———

Through the door that was beneath the sign that said "BAR," Henri took a seat at a table in the darkest corner of the place. Ronny Leroy was sitting at the farthest end of the bar, hunched over a glass. He never looked up when Henri entered.

One drink, two drinks, three. They were in their late forties, but Ronny looked like he was 60 — sapped by who-knew-what. Maybe the alcohol. Maybe pushing the wheelchair. Not that it mattered to Henri.

Four drinks. Other than using the toilet the one time, Ronny never moved. He never even sat up straight, and he didn't say a word to the bartender. He just signaled for another by pointing at the glass in front of him.

Five drinks, six — all in a little more than an hour. Henri had two glasses of wine as he waited and watched. He wasn't sure what he was going to do. In 1944, in the middle of an enemy occupation, surrounded by his friends, the blood of Mikey Leblanc still not washed off of the sidewalk by the rain — back then, he knew what he was going to do when they all arrived at 43 Rue Petrelle, only to find that Ronny and his mother had fled. Fifteen years later, though, he just wasn't sure. In fact, Henri was almost surprised — after he heard the scrape of the barstool, and watched Ronny Leroy, head down, trudge out the door — when he almost reflexively felt the pistol in its holster and then stood up and followed him.

B rown poison?
The one thing about Michel was his meticulousness, Martin thought. They met at Gérard's house pretty much every month, and each of them laid out the state of their piece of the business. He would talk about some stolen shipment of cognac from the other side of the Belgian border. Henri would tell the story of a consignment of Swiss watches that his boys had liberated after their arrival at Gare du Nord. And Michel? He was a traffic cop for the heroin gangs in Marseille, arranging transportation of the product out of Paris and into the port of New York. Mostly, it was New York. He stashed it inside of Citroen wheel-wells, and cases of champagne, and lately in shoe boxes that accompanied designer fashions and whatnot. But that's all it was — moving the product for a healthy fee, moving it to America. There was nothing in any of his reports about dealing

in Lourdes — which was, by the by, a lot closer to Marseille than it was to Paris.

A side deal, then? It must have been.

Secret from the family? Clearly.

You naughty boy, Martin thought, as one of the goons back-handed Michel off of the chair for what must have been the fourth time.

They were maybe five steps outside of the bar, and Henri came up to Ronny from behind and hugged him/pushed him into the alley they had reached. Ronny was drunk enough that his reaction was less of active resistance than of passive surprise. He stopped moving his feet, but that was the sum of his fight against Henri's push. The end result was that he tripped and fell to the cinders with Henri's final shove. And it was from his ass that he looked up at Henri, drunk and bewildered.

"You know who I am, right?" Henri said.

Ronny looked up. The alley was dark but not that dark. Henri could see him fine, and he knew Ronny could see him fine.

"Nothing?" Henri said. "Look closer."

With that, the two of them stared at each other, even if Ronny was drunk enough that, had it been a contest, he would have lost nine times out of 10. No, all 10. He was drunk, and shaken, and bewildered — but he stared. Henri said nothing. Then, after maybe 10 seconds, there was a flicker of recognition — a flicker, and then a drunken attempt to get to his feet. Henri halted the attempt by applying the bottom of his shoe to Ronny's chest and pushing. Hard.

It took Ronny a few seconds to recover. When he was sitting up again, Henri said, "Say it, Ronny."

Nothing.

"Say my name, Ronny."

Nothing again for maybe five more seconds. Only then did Ronny say a single word:

"Henri."

————

They picked up Michel and put him back on the chair, and Martin couldn't hear all of what the old man asked him, just snatches of a monologue, including, "You fuck with the lives of honest men and women, and you fuck your own family besides." It went on for a while, the volume dropping. Martin heard nothing of the last 10 seconds, but he heard the reply from his cousin. It was almost shouted.

"Fuck you, Big Tommy," Michel said. The words reverberated in the high-ceilinged space.

Two of the four men were holding guns on Michel, pistols. The other two — the old man and a younger kid — were empty-handed. Martin knew instinctively the proper order — pistols first, then the kid, then the old man. It wasn't as if he really had to think about it — and the "fuck you, Big Tommy" was his cue. Martin knew that instinctively, too. It was the family business, after all, and he had lived enough of it to know. He might spend most of his time peddling expensive champagne during the day and wearing a tuxedo at a gallery opening at night, but he knew. It was something you never forgot.

The whole thing took maybe 10 seconds, although he would replay it in his head later and it seemed like it took minutes. It was always like that, the memory in slow motion.

The first shot got one of the pistols in the back of the neck. The second shot, which was always going to be the toughest, got the other pistol in the face after he whirled around at the sound of the first shot. The third shot got the kid in the chest as he was fumbling to unbutton his jacket. The fourth shot got the old man, also in the chest. His mouth was wide open — in shock or wonder — when Martin pulled the trigger.

Michel had instinctively ducked when the shooting started, but he was sitting up again. He was sitting up, and only saw the last man standing a couple of seconds after the fourth shot.

"Evening, cousin," Martin said.

Then it was Michel with the wide-open mouth.

"We'll talk later," Martin said. "Plenty to talk about."

He paused.

"Plenty," Martin said.

There were four dead bodies on the floor, along with the briefcase. Martin looked down and saw that it contained three bricks of heroin, three kilos.

"Do we leave it?" Michel said.

"No offense, but that would be really fucking stupid, cousin," Martin said.

"Leave one brick?"

"Just as fucking stupid," Martin said. With that, he reached into his pocket and removed a pen knife. He took one brick from the briefcase and sliced through the paper. Then he stepped over one of the fallen bodies and sprinkled a bit of the heroin on the hands and in the lap of the dead kid. Then, for good measure, he sprinkled some more on the ground — maybe 100 grams worth. It looked like an ant hill.

"You want it to look like some kind of drug deal that went sideways," Martin said. "You leave the whole thing, it looks stupid. It makes no sense. This way, it's enough for the cops to find. They won't be able to fucking miss it, but they'll think they're geniuses. They'll have an easy answer and an extra beer for lunch."

Then Martin said, "And we keep the rest."

He put an emphasis on the word "we." And he stared at Michel when he said it. And when his cousin nodded and then his eyes dropped, Martin knew that he'd made his point. We.

W hen he thought about it later, he really believed he was going to leave Ronny in that alley — drunk, pathetic, pissing himself. He was done with his recitation and his denunciation, and if he didn't feel justice, he felt better — and if life and the last 15 years had taught Henri anything, it was that better was often the best you could do in a situation. That justice was a relative term. That perfect was a fantasy.

He was really going to leave him there in the alley, down in the cinders with a boot print on the front of his coat. He had even begun to turn to leave when Ronny said, quietly, "We really had no choice."

That was the trigger. That was it. Henri didn't even think when he heard the words, the feeble justification of every collaborator. He didn't ask for a further explanation. No thoughts, just reactions.

Henri reached for the gun, then considered the noise and the feeble pile of shit at his feet. He moved his hand from the holster to the breast pocket and pulled out the switchblade instead. Then he placed a knee on Ronny Leroy's chest to keep him in place. Ronny began crying.

"This is for Mikey Leblanc, whose children grew up without a father. And for the Resistance. And for France."

"But, my mother."

"Fuck your mother," Henri said, and then he shoved the knife in just below the ribs, just as his Uncle Gerard had showed him back when.

PART X

GROWING UP

Everybody seemed exhausted from the trip — Lemieux couldn't figure out why — and nobody was talking on the train ride back, nobody but Gérard. It had only been a couple of days, but you could already see the improvement. Whether or not his mental outlook was somehow boosting his physical condition, the priest had no idea. But there was little question that the old man was getting better. He was still tired, still napped, but his vigor in between the sleeps was unquestioned — and the color was returning to his face, at least a little.

They returned to Gérard's house in a taxi from the station, and the old man took another snooze in the chair that faced the Van Gogh. It was then that the priest went back to the kitchen and replaced the marmalade jars with two new ones — one orange, one peach, zero arsenic.

Later that night, Michel agreed to meet Martin in the garage where the rest of the heroin was stashed. Martin had been insistent, and Michel had been in no position to bargain — especially when Martin told him about the letter. They were standing outside the train toilets when Martin said, "I've written it all down in a letter — everything that went on last night. Every devious fucking bit of it. I posted it this morning from the hotel. You don't need to know where I sent it. All you need to know is that if anything happens to me, Gérard and Henri will have your thieving balls for lunch, you disloyal fuck."

Michel arrived first and left the garage door unlocked, the padlock hanging on the hasp. The truck with the tomato stenciled on the outside had been repainted black. The remaining heroin was hidden in the wall behind a big metal cabinet that held nails and screws and such. When Martin arrived, Michel could tell by the way he walked that he was at least half drunk. When he got close enough to smell, Michel adjusted the estimate to three-quarters.

But what was his play? The truth was, Michel couldn't think of one. Killing Martin was the obvious way to go, except for the letter. The family would barely miss him. Two weeks after the funeral, they would give the business to Freddy, and it would run just as smoothly, if not more. Martin really was a total fucking dope.

The letter might have been bullshit, but Michel couldn't take the chance. The total fucking dope not only had rescued him from Big Tommy Rheaume in Lourdes, but he had also had the foresight to write the insurance policy and post it from the hotel. That was the worst part of it in some ways, being outsmarted by Martin, by the total fucking dope. But there it was.

"So, how much more do you have?" Martin said. So much for pleasantries.

"Three bricks."

"Fucking liar."

"Three bricks, I promise," Michel said. In truth, there were 12 more kilos of heroin hidden in the wall, but Michel was sure that his face betrayed no such thing.

"Liar," Martin said. And then he looked around and saw a wooden desk chair and plopped his three-quarters drunken ass down into it.

"But, it doesn't really matter," Martin said. "However many bricks you have left, you lying fuck, does not concern me."

Michel had figured that Martin's play would be to demand a percentage of the illicit heroin trade for as long as it lasted. He thought that Martin would start by asking for something like 70-30 in his favor, and then Michel would do his best to talk him down toward 50-50. They would shake hands, and Michel would eat the shit sandwich, and that would be that. The upside would be that any kind of deal like that would mean that Martin was in the illicit heroin business, too. That would offer at least a tiny layer of protection to Michel if the others found out.

But Martin had obviously thought that through, too.

"This is how we're going to play it," he said. "I saved your ass, and if anybody in the family ever asks, I'm going to say that you told me that it was because those Rheaumes were making noise about interrupting shipments from Marseille that went through their territory, and that you resisted, and that they made a move, and well..."

Martin stopped talking and belched. The fumes could have fueled a jet airliner.

"If there's a hole in the story, well, my uncle and my brother think I'm an idiot anyway, right?" Martin said.

Michel didn't answer, didn't move a facial muscle.

"So, here's how it'll go," Martin said. "You run your disloyal fucking side business however you want — I really don't care. But at the end of the quarter, I will take half of your kick from the family pot. I'll know exactly how much it is, because I get the same amount. And you'll take half of your envelope and give it to me. Maybe we'll do it right here in this garage, four times a year. Make a ceremony out of it, like in the back room at Vincent's. Yeah, just like that — but without Silent Moe in the background."

Again, Michel said nothing as Martin stood up, toppled the wooden chair in the process, and shuffled to the garage door and out. Michel was cornered and he knew it. He couldn't believe it, but his three-quarters drunken cousin had it all figured out. The total fucking dope.

Raymond Ruel, a man with a back so hairy that it likely kept him warm in the cold weather, had just left Clarice's apartment. She was naked beneath the covers, lost in thought — but not about Ruel's looks (average), penis (below average), technique (enthusiastic), wife (homely), or about the winter coat that crept up to his shoulders. It was the rest of it, the reason she had cultivated the relationship. Coffee the first time, drinks the second, dinner the third, dinner and then the bedroom on the fourth, fifth, and sixth. This night was the sixth, and Clarice figured it was time.

Ruel's family owned a wholesale flour business. "We grow it and we grind it," Raymond said, and it was the largest such business in France. His father had taken the company public about 10 years earlier, and now Raymond was the chief executive officer. It was a big job for a 30-year-old, but he had his father's help when he needed it.

"But he gives me my head," Raymond said. "He's barely around anymore. I've grown into the job, if I do say so myself."

He talked like that, in between the sex. Very impressed with himself, Raymond was. Clarice listened, and acted as if she was impressed, and waited for the opening. This night, the sixth night, was when it came.

They had both regained their breath, and Raymond was talking about how he sat at the head of the table at the board meetings that his father didn't attend, and Clarice said, "The power, it must be, I don't know, intoxicating."

"I like to think I'm level-headed."

"I know, I know. It's just that, the opportunities for the easiest money must present themselves every day."

"Easy money? Nothing's easy about the flour business. Growing and grinding and bagging and delivering — it's hard work. Not easy. Not easy money at all. A drought affects the bottom line. Petrol prices affect the bottom line. Labor issues — not easy. Not easy money at all. Well, until..."

"What do you mean?"

"Our secret, right?"

She caressed him down there and said, "Of course. Of course."

At which point, Raymond Ruel, CEO, revealed the news that had been percolating for at least three months. That was when Clarice first heard it, just a whisper of it — from the man who ran her neighborhood bakery in the 6th, of all people. He said he heard it from one of the delivery drivers. That is, that the Ruels — already the biggest in the industry — were considering buying out the Favells, who were No. 3. The Ruels dominated the Paris region, and the Favells owned Bordeaux. The biggest would become bigger — and the price, the driver told the baker, was more than fair because Mr. Favell had just died and Mrs. Favell wanted nothing to do with grinding wheat. Oh, and she was 83.

"But how can the driver know that?" Clarice said, and the baker told her in a whisper: "Because the driver knows one of the Favell granddaughters." He put a special emphasis on the word "knows."

And now, Clarice knew. It was from that hint, that whisper, that she began to stalk Ruel. And now, in her bed, he was telling her that the deal was done. The cost savings from the combined operation would be enormous, Raymond said. She had two weeks before the announcement that would likely cause the price of Ruel shares to increase by 20 percent in a day.

———

Henri parked the car, a recently stolen blue Citroen with a dent in the left rear fender, about 200 feet from the house on Avenue Dutuit. When Lucien Richard headed over to his art gallery to open for the day, this was the way he would walk.

Henri sat in the driver's seat and unrolled the passenger side window. It would be an easy shot.

The pistol sat beside him on the bench front seat. He looked at it, picked it up, felt its heft, then put it back down again.

He looked ahead to Richard's front door, then down at the gun. Front door, gun. Front door, gun.

What the hell was he doing?

He thought back and tried to remember the last time he had killed two people in a week. Had he ever done it, outside of the Resistance years? Henri couldn't remember. Then again, he couldn't really focus. And, well, forget two in a week. When was the last time he had killed two men in a year? Better yet — when was the last time he had killed a man, a single man, for anything other than a business reason?

He looked at his watch: 9:40. The gallery opened in 20 minutes and was a 10-minute walk away, give or take. It had to be soon. He picked up the newspaper and pretended to read it as he looked over the top. Still no movement at Richard's front door.

Sylvie had been there two days before. The private detective had provided the tick-tock — in the door, out the door, three hours in between. Based on how she was dressed for breakfast — crappy dress, almost no makeup — and how she said she would have to wait around until the upholstery guy brought back the stained dining room chair, Henri was fairly certain that she did not have a visit to Avenue Dutuit planned for that morning.

His watch again: 9:44.

Other than Ronny Leroy, Henri couldn't remember a personal killing. Vengeful killings, yes — but always for a business reason, some kind of payback, soldier to soldier. Unfortunate killings, yes — but always in the midst of some sort of criminal enterprise. Never just for the hell of it. Never to settle some kind of personal score. And if Ronny Leroy had elements of just that, he also was a traitor to his people in wartime. Collaborators were still being tried and jailed 15 years later, so they could be executed, too. So, it was personal but it wasn't. Not like this.

His watch again: 9:46.

What the fuck was he doing? Why was this different than the butcher, Jack Quillette — you know, other than that his own dick wasn't working properly anymore? Henri and Sylvie had a detente of sorts when it came to this stuff, unspoken and long-standing, like in so many other marriages. As long as it wasn't shoved in the face of the other, there was, well, tolerance.

Henri had had a girlfriend since the third year of their marriage. That seemed to be the accepted period of time. How did Passy put it? "There are 24 hours in a day, 24 months of faithfulness. I think it's in the Bible, 24. It's a holy number."

To which Timmy replied, "Where in the Bible? Saint Paul's letter to the Pussyhounds?"

Henri didn't know when Sylvie and the butcher started, but it was after that. And given his ability to read her moods, it wasn't all that often — a couple of times a year, maybe.

So, what was it about this guy?

Just then, Lucien Richard came out and turned toward Henri's parked blue Citroen with the dented fender. Still peering over the newspaper, Henri reached over and picked up the gun. He held the newspaper with his left hand and the gun with his right hand. It was heavier than normal because of the silencer. He felt the weight where he rested it on his right thigh.

Richard walked quickly.

A hundred feet away.

Fifty.

Twenty-five.

Richard never looked over at the blue Citroen.

Ten feet.

Five.

Richard was looking at his wristwatch as he passed the open window on the passenger side. Henri raised the gun — or, rather, began to raise it. Two, three inches maybe. Not six inches. Definitely not six.

And then, for whatever reason — and not because he was worried about getting caught, because Avenue Dutuit was quiet — Henri laid the gun back on the bench seat, and Lucien Richard continued on his walk to work.

———

G uy had been anxious about the lunch since his father called. It was at Gartner's, his father's regular lunch place, around the corner from the uniform business that provided pretty much everyone in the family with a paycheck and a tax identification number for the government. His father was already halfway through the bread basket when Guy walked in.

"I'm not late," he said.

"I didn't say you were," Henri said.

"It's just," Guy said, pointing at the bread basket.

"I was hungry."

The father shrugged. He looked a bit off, but Guy had no idea why. Maybe it was just the whole business of the Pink

Ballet. Or, rather, what they were going to have to do about the Pink Ballet. Guy's mind had wandered into all of the dark places while he waited for his father to call. All of the dark places, every one of them.

They ordered — Salad Niçoise without the egg for Henri, Croque Monsieur for Guy — and talked about Lourdes while they waited for the food. In Guy's experience, Henri was a church-by-tradition kind of Catholic rather than the church-by-belief sort, and his father did nothing to dispel the notion. Like, when he said, "Let's just say that the guy who helped me off with my drawers seemed a lot more interested in what was underneath than in my fucking salvation."

"Might have been your imagination," Guy said.

"Don't think so."

"And did Gérard get naked with his best priest buddy?"

"I don't think so," Henri said. "I don't know. But I really think you're wrong about that."

"Guilty until proven innocent."

"What, that's the new definition of justice?"

"Open your eyes," Guy said.

The food came and Henri changed the direction of the conversation to the business of the bordellos, and Guy was happy enough to report on the relatively smooth operations, and the slowly increasing profits.

"You've seen the envelopes," Guy said.

"I have. They're good. It looks like you were right about the improvements at the skank place. That's where the growth is?"

"Slowly, but yeah," Guy said. It probably wasn't the first time his father had used the phrase "you were right" in a conversation with his son, but it was the first time Guy could remember. It took everything he had not to grin when he heard it.

"You need any help with the operations? Another man or two?"

"I think we're good," Guy said. "I mean, it really isn't that hard. I have a checklist for the week, and I work my way through it, and both places run fine. Checklist in the afternoon, and then it's just a matter of hanging around, being there in case. I can hang around."

"Never doubted that part," Henri said, and then he smiled. "But it can be a long day, and there will come a time when it's too long a day. Like, when you have a regular girl or a family. Anything happening there?"

"No regular girl. And no, abso-fucking-lutely no family."

Henri just smiled again, and then he began a serious assault on the Salad Niçoise, and then he said, "Now, the other thing."

The other thing.

Here we go, Guy thought.

"Still nothing else in the papers?" Henri said.

"Not since what I showed you."

"You sure?"

"Every paper, every day. I'm sure."

"And have you talked to your boy?"

"Day before yesterday, yeah," Guy said. "Still nothing."

"He hasn't been questioned?"

"No questions, no appointment yet. But he thinks it's coming. I asked him about the other guys on the list from the newspaper, and he said two of them had been in to be questioned for sure."

His father went back to the salad. For his part, Guy had managed to choke down about a quarter of his sandwich. They were sitting at a corner table, Henri's regular table. The next-closest patrons were 20 feet away.

"I've been thinking about it," his father said. "And, the more I think about it, the more I believe that your boy is a loose end that we can't afford. You know, for all of the reasons I explained before."

"The publicity?"

"The publicity, yeah. You see the papers — there's still a story almost every day. At least in *France-Soir*, there is."

"In most of them," Guy said.

"So, you see. This is such a thing now — your mother grabs the paper from me if I have it first, just to read the latest. It seems clear the cops are in it, at least on the fringes, and they hate that for all of the obvious reasons. So, if they can get the La Rue family involved in it..."

"Barely involved," Guy said.

"Doesn't matter. Barely involved will be good enough for them to pump it beyond all reality. And it could shut us down for months. If the cops were drowning, we would be their lifeline."

"In the papers."

"Exactly, in the papers. Suddenly, the story every day will be about some bullshit La Rue organization arrest or some foiled warehouse robbery or..."

Henri's voice trailed off.

"And every story will have our involvement in the Pink Ballet scandal in the second paragraph. And that makes for one less story about the cops being involved. I'm telling you, it could be months. Your places would be shut down in a blink. The protection and information we pay the cops for at Gare du Nord — over."

"You don't think we could survive with, well, with bigger payoffs?" Guy said.

"That's a good thought," Henri said. He speared a stray piece of tuna from the salad that barely fit into his mouth.

"A good thought," his father said. "But I don't think it would work. The pressure would be enormous from the brass. Our guys — the guys we pay — some of them are just survivors but a lot of them are ambitious. They can't ignore their bosses any more than anyone in any business can ignore their boss. Not for long, anyway."

Henri took some bread, and wiped the dressing off of the plate, and chewed noisily.

"Not hungry?"

"Bigger breakfast than I should have," Guy said.

Henri shrugged, wiped, and chewed.

"I'll stand in the way and block the view if you want to lick the plate."

"Smart ass — I didn't have the egg."

The father laughed. The son smiled.

"A loose end, we just can't have it," Henri said. And then he went on to explain the plan he had concocted, the where and the when and the how. It was simple and neat. At one point, his father explained, "Simple is the best. Always as simple as you can make it. When there's trouble, it's almost always because you got too cute. You know, like..."

"Like the clown masks," Guy said. It wasn't that long ago that Guy's burgeoning career as a bank robber was foiled because of the disguises he and his men wore at an otherwise perfect robbery. The problem wasn't that they were clown masks. It was that they were expensive clown masks that could be purchased at only two costume shops in the city — and that he had run his mouth when he was buying them, besides.

"Yeah, like that," Henri said. Again, he smiled. Some fathers taught their sons to fish, Guy thought. Then there was Henri La Rue.

Henri talked some more, going over the details, the where, and the when, and the how. But he never got to the part that was keeping his son up at night, the detail that was robbing Guy of his appetite.

The where, and the when, and the how — but not the who. He never got to the part about who would be pulling the trigger.

C larice had tried and failed and couldn't figure another way. The two weeks before the announcement of the Ruel acquisition had shrunk to five days, and her plan was no closer to fruition. The problem was that she needed some leverage because the 20 percent gain on the Ruel shares wouldn't be enough to satisfy her agreement with the family. The only way to get that leverage — the ability to buy on margin and multiply the gain — was to involve someone with a seat on the bourse. Those brokerages were the only ones big enough to handle the transaction and to hide it among the rest of their business — and it had to be hidden. Buying a couple of hundred shares in Ruel in the days leading up to the acquisition would be considered dumb luck. Buying a hundred thousand shares would not — especially if the regulators bothered to notice the name La Rue on the order tickets.

So, a broker with a seat on the bourse. Most of them were old-school boy scouts who would throw her out of the office at the first hint of a dirty deal. From what she had gathered, just listening to the gossiping that took place at The Crane after the closing bell every afternoon, there was a name that provoked more arched eyebrows than any other when it came up. Delhomme. François Delhomme. Fast Frankie. Arched eyebrow.

But Fast Frankie turned her down. Clarice went to his office and laid out her idea — without mentioning the Ruel shares specifically — and he shook his head. He said, "Two reasons. One, because the regulators also know that people call me Fast Frankie — and your scheme is just too basic, too easy to spot if they know where to look."

"But it's not illegal."

"It's unethical. It's frowned upon."

"You wouldn't go to jail."

"I could lose my seat," Delhomme said. "Or, at the least, get marginalized. Like you need me, I sometimes need those stuffy assholes from the oldest families."

"What's two, the second reason?" Clarice said.

"Two, you don't trust me enough to share the name of the shares in question. I'm not going to risk getting fucked by the regulators if you can't show me a basic level of trust."

"You'll know on the day."

"I need to know earlier if I'm to benefit appropriately."

"But if you buy it up early, my profit shrinks. The truth is, if I tell you early, you could take the information and fuck me entirely."

"No risk, no reward," Delhomme said. He shrugged, and then he banged his fountain pen on the desk. Once. Twice. "But even then, the regulators. It's just not a good time. I can't."

And that was where they had left it. Three days had passed, and only five remained until the announcement, and Clarice couldn't think of another play. So she made the phone call she had been dreading all along, the phone call to her father.

Henri was somewhere between intrigued and shocked when the phone call from his daughter came. They didn't talk on the phone — didn't talk much, period — and they certainly didn't have lunch, just the two of them. Certainly not at her invitation.

They met over on her side of the Seine, and they began a meandering walk in and around the Latin Quarter. He greeted her with an awkward hug, and she mumbled something about a café she liked, and then they were walking. Walking and not really talking, other than about the weather (tolerable, they agreed) and the traffic on Boulevard Saint-Germain (horrendous, they agreed). Then it was up a side street, uphill, up. They were near the top when Clarice pointed to a building on the right.

"Hemingway and his wife lived there, 74 Rue du Cardinal Lemoine. His first wife, I think. But I guess I don't really know."

She didn't tell her father that Pierre's place was in the same building. She thought of him as her boyfriend, at least when her mind wandered, even though neither of them saw a long term for them. She didn't tell him about the toilet down the hall from Pierre's place, and how he said, "You've shit on the same toilet that Hemingway did. Makes you tingle just thinking about it, doesn't it?"

Instead, her father jumped in.

"I knew Hemingway, you know," Henri said.

"You what?

Knew Hemingway? Knew the great Hemingway? Like, really knew?"

"Not knew, not actually. But met. Met and spent several hours getting drunk with him. You think he's a great writer. I'll tell you, he's a great drinker."

"Wait a minute — you left the butte? You?"

"I was young once, and I was like you — I thought the butte was a jail sometimes. My father, it was always 'Montmartre this,' and 'Montmartre that,' and 'the butte this,' and 'the butte that.' We lived there, worked there — and sometimes, you wanted more. You know? Not anymore, but when you're young..."

With that, Henri told her the story of drinking at the Ritz when the city was liberated, and the Nazis were pushed out, and the wildly uproarious scene in the city. He and his brothers all made their way down the hill and participated in the revelry. He didn't tell Clarice about the reveler named Amanda that the three La Rue brothers shared that night, in age order, in the alley behind the hotel. But he did tell her about Hemingway commanding the Ritz bar like a general, ordering the help around, paying for either everything or nothing — Henri was never sure.

"I can't believe I never heard that story," she said, after he was finished.

"I can't remember the last time I told it," Henri said, and he wasn't lying. It had probably been a decade, at least. And then he remembered why he didn't like telling it — because of Amanda in the alley, and what she said when Martin got his turn after Little Jean and Henri: "Ah, ah, ah, the best for last."

They walked past the Hemingway house and about 100 feet away was a little square where five streets met. Henri did a quick count — five, six, no seven restaurants faced the square.

He looked around and said, "You know, I'm not really hungry."

"Neither am I."

"Let's just..." Henri pointed at the little fountain in the middle of the square. It was surrounded by small benches. They grabbed the last available bench on the sunny, cold day. At least there was no wind. Tolerable.

"So," Henri said, and then he waited. It was her ask, and now he would wait for her. They watched a little boy reaching a stick into the fountain and making little splashes.

"Well," Clarice said. And then, after as much time as was required to take a deep breath, she told him everything — about the Ruel shares, and the need for the assistance of a broker with a seat on the bourse, and the reluctance of Fast Frankie, and the ticking clock. Well, not everything — she didn't tell her father about Ruel's equipment (below average), or his technique (enthusiastic), or about his hairy back.

"And from me you need, what from Ruel—"

"No, not Ruel. From Fast Frankie."

"Some what? Some, how do you say, encouragement?"

"Well..."

"Some encouragement from your old dad?"

Clarice nodded and looked down. He sensed the humiliation

she felt because of having to ask for his help. He could tell how it hurt her, how it made her feel like a child. And part of him really liked it, all of it. He had never wanted her in the business. And if he had been impressed with her first scheme, the franc devaluation thing, part of him thought it was a one-off, just luck. Part of him believed she wasn't cut out for the rest of it, the relentlessness of the family business. He knew that the La Rue family was about money a lot more than it was about family, and he wasn't sure she could stomach it.

And, so, he liked it, this bit of groveling — but, maybe, not enough to rub it in her face. Besides, it also dawned on him — very quickly — that his daughter might be able to provide him with a service, too.

"This guy, this broker," Henri said.

"François Delhomme. Fast Frankie."

"Whatever. Besides your thing, can he do something else?"

"Something for you?"

Henri nodded.

"Can he, I don't know, frame someone?" he said.

"Frame someone for what?"

"I don't know, dirty trading, securities fraud, I'm not sure what you call it."

"Maybe. Probably. Can I ask why?"

"No."

"If you won't tell me, I can't help you."

"You're not in much of a position to bargain, young lady."

"Yet, here I am, bargaining anyway," she said.

Henri laughed. And then, he told her. He wasn't sure what had come over him, but he just told her. When he thought about it later, part of him couldn't believe how he had unburdened himself to the daughter who had butted heads with him for years. It was personal, and it was embarrassing, and it was something that no one else on earth knew — no one. Yet, he told her anyway. He started, and the words just tumbled out without emotion or embarrassment. That surprised him, too.

Henri told Clarice everything about Lucien Richard and her mother. He told her every bit of it — well, not about his dick but all of the rest, including sitting in his car along the curb in front of Richard's apartment building, peering over the newspaper and fingering the gun on the car seat next to him, then lifting it and feeling its heft. If she was going to be in, she might as well understand what she was dealing with.

PART XI

AN ELEGANT SOLUTION

P hilip Tanguay was drunk on a bench in the Gare du Nord, drunk with the other two. It was 4:30 a.m., and he was half awake and half sober, more or less. The cops didn't bother to clear out the station platforms overnight, mostly because there were always a couple of legitimate people who were waiting for the milk runs to Lille and Metz, waiting and dozing on the benches. A few drunks mixed in didn't do anyone any harm, provided they weren't hassling anyone or bellowing or throwing up. Philip and his mates were doing none of those things. One was snoring, but not obnoxiously.

They had been at a club somewhere in the 10th because of the band and the women it attracted. That was the reputation, anyway, but it turned out to be bullshit. The Rarifieds were a shit three-piece jazz combo, and the women were cows, and the only logical alternative was to drink the bar dry. Which they did. How they had ended up in the Gare du Nord was a bit hazy, not that it mattered. The Metro would be open in a bit, and then bed.

In his stupor — well, semi-stupor at best — Philip heard of the opportunity before he saw it. There were two men in black uniforms, both with pistols in holsters on their hips, and they were talking as they passed the bench where the three of them were sleeping off the night before. Philip didn't open his eyes and see them until he had heard them first, heard the guy on the left in particular when he said, "What do you figure? A million?"

"After the bank holiday? Easy." That was the answer from the guy on the right.

The two of them walked to the very end of the platform and waited for a train that arrived at 4:38. It was a normal train, pretty empty, but there were three cars at the end painted blue. They were the cars dedicated to mail delivery, it seemed, given the stylized logo of La Poste that was stenciled on the side of the cars.

The other two slept while Philip watched through slitted

eyes. The departing passengers cleared the platform quickly, which left the two men with the pistols on their hips way down at the end. A door of one of the mail cars opened, and one of the men was given a clipboard to sign, and then both of the men were handed something. Then they began walking toward the bench on their return. They were taking their time, chatting and laughing — Philip could see that from the beginning. When they got to within about 400 feet, he could see that each was carrying a black valise as they walked.

A million?

Would a million fit in two valises?

Philip looked around, turning his head ever so slightly. Through the slits, he saw one old man asleep on a bench, three benches down. Beyond that, nothing. If the men carrying the valises had helpers, they weren't obvious. If Philip had to guess, they had an armored car parked at the curb outside the station — maybe with a driver inside, maybe not. But if there was anyone else inside, they weren't on the platform.

Three hundred feet.

Two hundred feet.

The two guys were carrying the valises with their right hands. The pistols were strapped to their right hips. Idiots.

Philip felt the baby pistol in his pants pocket. He always carried it, even if his grandfather made fun of it. The old man would say, "Tiny gun, tiny dick," and laugh with his old buddies, but Philip still carried it everywhere, and fuck Sleepy-fucking-JoJo. He was pretty sure his grandfather had never scored a million francs in a single job, not in his whole wasted fucking life.

One hundred feet.

Fifty feet.

The two guys with the pistols on their hips were talking loudly enough to be heard at that point. The one guy was telling

a story of some sort and laughing, and the other guy was interrupting him with the repeated mantra, "Total fucking bullshit."

He said it once, twice, three times.

And then Philip stood and fired. Once, twice.

The shots both were on target. He aimed for their chests
and, even drunk, made reasonably accurate contact. The one
guy got it in the neck and looked dead. The other was shot lower
— belly or balls — and was sprawled on the platform, sprawled
and screaming.

The noise woke Philip's two mates in a burst of frantic what-
the-fucks. Philip grabbed both valises and sprinted. He yelled,
"Come on," and the other two joined him. They headed down a
side ramp from the platform — not into the main station but
into the bowels of the place, near the toilets and the left luggage.
There would be an exit out to the street down there somewhere.
That's what Philip was figuring when a single shot fired from
behind them. It must have been the belly/balls guy. Philip
ducked but kept running. He turned long enough to see that his
snoring companion had been hit, and a pool of blood was
already forming around his head. His name was Rocco.

Henri collected François Delhomme outside of his office
after the stock and bond markets closed. He had thought
about bringing along some help but ultimately figured that if he
couldn't make a fucking stockbroker get into his car, well, then
he was in the wrong business. As if turned out, the outline of the
pistol in his jacket pocket was more than enough.

He had Delhomme drive, even though the man was crying.
The destination was a garage in the 9th in which the La Rues
stored various vehicles that came into their possession, legally
and otherwise. They were there in about 15 minutes, but only

because of the traffic. The distance between the bourse and the garage wasn't two miles.

Clarice was waiting in the garage when they arrived.

"You've met my father," she said.

Fast Frankie was a little slow on the uptake, but then he made the connection. He knew her last name was La Rue, but if it wasn't a common surname, it wasn't uncommon, either. He had not made the connection, not until that moment. And then, he cried some more.

"In the chair, now," Henri said.

Delhomme obeyed.

"Good man," Henri said. Meanwhile, Clarice walked over and sat on a chair of her own against the far wall, maybe 30 feet away. She could see and hear everything, but the distance was the distance.

Delhomme was not only crying while he sat there, but he also had pissed himself. The suit he wore was light gray, and you could see the mess in his lap before you could smell it. Henri stared until he saw a few drops of urine fall from his left pant leg and onto the cinder floor. Time to begin then.

Henri explained, "I understand that my daughter has come to you with a proposition, but that you have resisted." Then he slapped Delhomme on the cheek with the back of his hand. The ring he wore would leave a mark, but it wasn't bad. It really wasn't much of a slap at all.

Still, Delhomme wailed. It was a pretty loud scream, but no one on the street would be able to hear. Besides, it was just the one. After that came the blubbering, loud but not shouted — a maelstrom of "I can't" and "the regulators" and "my business" and "I could lose everything."

Henri listened for about a minute as he took off his coat and rolled up his sleeves. And then, with his bare right elbow, he broke Delhomme's nose and neatly sidestepped the blood spray.

Clarice watched her father's pirouette and thought, "I guess he's done this before." At the same time, Henri stole a peek and watched her watching. What struck him was the intensity that showed on her face — not horror, not revulsion, but intensity. She didn't flinch, didn't blink. She just watched.

And Fast Frankie wailed again — longer this time, but only a little. Then he was quiet. He watched as Henri walked about 20 feet over to a work table and picked up a hammer. He picked it up, and lightly hit his open palm with it, once, twice, three times. He looked at the hammer, and at his palm, and then he turned and made eye contact with Delhomme as he began walking back toward the blood-stained, piss-stained, tear-stained little man.

Henri counted, and Delhomme was agreeing to everything by the third step. The only surprise was that it took that long. Henri said that Delhomme and Clarice would work out the details, and if things went satisfactorily, he would never visit Delhomme again. Henri handed Fast Frankie a handkerchief, and Delhomme went about tidying his face. Then, he said, "But what will I tell my wife?"

"Tell her you walked into a door," Henri said.

Then, after Delhomme was done wiping — it really wasn't that much blood — Henri said, "But I have one more request."

———

S ylvie was out when Henri arrived back at the apartment. He thought that maybe she was with Lucien Richard, but the notion didn't sicken him, not after what he had just set up with Fast Frankie. Henri even smiled when he thought it.

Shower, beer, newspaper — in that order. It was at the kitchen table where he found that day's copy of *France-Soir*. Sylvie had already read it, and the sections were all pulled apart.

It was only when Henri restored some order that he saw the headline on the front page. Well, he more than saw it because the headline screamed at him:

DARING MAIL TRAIN ROBBERY AT GARE DU NORD

And, the smaller headline:

Two dead, 1 million francs stolen

Henri read the article quickly — it wasn't very long — and got the gist: the train was hit before 5 a.m., one of the guards was killed, another wounded, and one of the three thieves was killed. Nobody was identified.

His first thought was, "Fucking Freddy." Henri slammed down the newspaper and walked over to the telephone in the hallway. Sylvie had taken three messages from Freddy — each marked "important" — and a fourth message from Mr. Brown. That one was marked "urgent" and specified a meeting at 6 p.m. Henri checked his watch. He still had time.

He called Freddy and before he could say anything, all he heard in the receiver was "It wasn't me and it wasn't us, boss. I fucking swear."

"Are you fucking sure?"

"Boss, I'm sure."

"But some of those assholes you have––"

"I'm sure, boss. It wasn't us. I swear on my mother."

"Your mother's been dead since the war."

"I fucking swear, boss. It wasn't us."

Henri and Gérard both had been adamant when the La Rues got control of the Gare du Nord: no mail trains. Freddy had said they were probably lucrative, and Henri didn't disagree, but no. The complications were just not worth the benefits. Too much else would be jeopardized by a mail train robbery. It was a federal crime, for one, and the publicity alone could be crippling — and Freddy listened. At least, Henri thought he did —

and listening on the phone, he believed what Freddy was telling him.

"So?" Henri said.

"No fucking idea," Freddy said.

"None?"

"The Levines?"

"I can't imagine — they have their own station," Henri said. "To come over to ours, it would be such a clear violation. Besides, they could end up in the same shit, too. Christ, the two stations are only a few blocks apart."

Henri was on time for the 6 p.m. meeting, but Chrétien was waiting for him, pacing and looking at his watch, when he arrived at the little park on Rue Burq.

"Christ, you've really fucking done it this time," the policeman said.

"Wasn't us, Chrétien."

"Like hell."

"Wasn't us, I swear."

"Regardless," Chrétien said, and then he went on to explain the ramifications — not that Henri required an explanation. Because of the mail train robbery, the Gare du Nord was now what the cop called "a frozen zone." It didn't matter what the La Rues had been paying the cops, all deals were off — at least temporarily. Nobody in a uniform would be looking the other way on anything, including spitting on one of the train platforms. The heat from above was just too intense.

"And that goes for the Gare de l'Est, too," Chrétien said.

"You don't think they?"

"La Rues, Levines, I don't fucking know and I almost don't fucking care. But nobody's going to be doing any business out of either station for a while."

"Define a while."

"Weeks."

"Like two weeks or 10 weeks?"

"Four or five, if I had to guess. Depends on the newspapers, mostly — or if we catch them quicker than that."

"Four or five weeks — that's a fucking lot," Henri said, and Chrétien's response was a shrug. At that point, Henri asked the cop if he knew anything about the dead thief. He said the kid's name was Rocco Myre, and that he was 21 years old, and lived in a shithole on Rue Lacaze, and was nowhere to be found in any police records.

"Not so much as a parking ticket," Chrétien said.

It was only when Henri went home, and looked at the Paris atlas, that he saw where Rue Lacaze was. In the 14th arrondissement.

***

Gérard hung up the phone and turned to Father Lemieux. "You heard?"

"The basics, yes."

"The basics are plenty," Gérard said.

It was past 7 p.m., and Silent Moe had already gone home for dinner with his wife. It was at that time of day when Gérard enjoyed having the priest around, even if they were just reading separately in the same room and not really talking.

"I'm just feeling so much better," is what the old man said, nearly on the hour, every hour. After lunch that day, Gérard had gone through an elaborate speech of thanks and appreciation to Lemieux — thanks for insisting he travel to Lourdes, thanks for the strength of his faith.

"And my faith, it seems to get stronger in your presence — some kind of synergy," Gérard said.

"It's your faith, Gérard, not mine," Lemieux said.

"That's bullshit, Jean — you should excuse the expression. You feed my faith. You nourish my soul."

They talked some more, and Lemieux looked more than he listened. Alain Benneville had been so right about the arsenic, about both the effects of its ingestion and the effects of its withdrawal. Gérard already looked 10 years younger than he had in the previous few months, younger and more robust.

"You do the books already," Gérard said. "I would like you around more often, for consultation, for counsel. You know what I mean?"

"I'm already around a lot."

"Can you move in?"

"I'm already pretty much moved in, Gérard."

"I mean, more. Completely. You seem, how can I put it, underemployed by the archdiocese? Am I right? You could still keep your room in the rectory, right? And for your weekly meeting with the cardinal, every Friday, right? Well, you could stay down there on Thursday nights, I guess — but it's a short ride. Besides that, really, what else is there? You look at the cardinal's books before the meeting, but you don't keep the books anymore? Right? You have people for that. They prepare the reports, you massage them a little and then report to the big man. Yes?"

"Pretty much," the priest said. This was going so well, he had to work to keep from appearing excited.

"I need Thursday in the office, all day, and Friday morning before the meeting with the cardinal. And the occasional dinner meeting, or other obligation. But..."

"Other than that..." Gérard said.

"Other than that, perhaps. Yes, perhaps."

That was where they had left it. After dinner, and the phone call from Henri about the mail train at the Gare du Nord, and the "frozen zone" for the next month at least, Gérard said he wasn't sure what to do — that he had a thought, but he wasn't positive.

"So, Jean?"

"I think you have to talk to the Levines," the priest said, and Gérard smiled.

"It's what I was thinking — but I hesitated," he said. "I hesitate more than I used to. My instincts are still right — but I have trouble pulling the trigger, at least sometimes. I have trouble, more and more. Old age, I guess."

Gérard reached for his brandy and took a small sip.

"I need you here. I need you by my side."

And Jean Lemieux again had to summon every ounce of his self-control to keep from bursting into a grin.

———

In the end, the whole thing went exactly as Clarice had imagined. François Delhomme, wearing a bit of foundation to cover the bruise on his left cheek and sort of cover the black eyes, took the information and made the trades, as instructed. In exchange for allowing him a measure of participation in the outcome — a piece of her piece — Fast Frankie permitted her to use three times leverage on the transaction, which was high but not unheard of for valued clients. How he hid it all within the books was his problem, and she didn't ask any questions. And on the day of the Ruel company announcement, she had him sell the position for a 24 percent gain — and that was after legitimate commissions and her under-the-table payment to Delhomme. With triple leverage, she had just increased the La Rue money by 72 percent, more than 3.5 million francs.

Clarice was explaining all of this to her father on the telephone that night. Except she told him the gain was only 62 percent. The extra 500,000 francs would be heading into her private account, and no one in the family would be the wiser. She was well over the 50 percent requirement, after all, and it wasn't as if anybody was going to be doing an audit.

Her father congratulated her, and Clarice went out of her way to say, "I couldn't have done it without you." It was the political thing to say but it also was the truth. She could tell by the quick catch in her father's voice that it had been on target.

"And the rest?" Henri said. "Did your Fast Frankie take care of the rest?"

"Read the paper tomorrow."

And the next day, on the front page of *France-Soir*, the biggest headline was about the arrest of an art dealer named Lucien Richard for securities fraud. Henri was reading the paper in his office. He had gone in early, while Sylvie was still in bed.

Besides Richard, the name of broker François Delhomme was all over the story, too. From what he could tell, Delhomme was portraying himself as an innocent victim taken in by Richard's connection to his parish church. Henri wondered if the cops would buy it and if Delhomme was going to lose his seat on the bourse if they didn't. But he only wondered about it for a second.

Henri read the story once, and then he read it a second time, and then he just stared at the front page. The more he looked at it, the more he had to admit that the gigantic photograph taken outside of the gallery, the subject in handcuffs, did not do Lucien Richard justice. He really was a handsome man.

PART XII

FATHERS AND SONS

"Let's blow off some steam — my treat," Guy said when he called Serge Lemelin. And if Lemelin was seemingly paralyzed by fear that he would be brought in for questioning about the Pink Ballet, well, a night at Trinity One might be just the tonic.

When Lemelin arrived, Guy was waiting outside for him, outside the BNCI bank branch that was on the first floor of the building that faced Trinity Church. Trinity One was on the second and third floors, casino and bordello. Guy offered the casino, but Lemelin demurred.

"Just whisky and pussy tonight, and not necessarily in that order," Lemelin said. "My God, I am so stressed out."

Guy got Lemelin situated with Celeste, his current favorite. He didn't let on, but he was too nervous himself, so it would be only whisky for him. To make it look good, though, he did take a shower and put on one of the plush cotton robes that the customers seemed to love. They all wore them when they had their after-sex drinks — that is, unless they were in a hurry to get either home or down to the casino. There were no robes at the whorehouses that Guy ran, and that was only one of the differences between them and Trinity One. The alcohol was top shelf. The air smelled of a hint of vanilla. Even the guys working behind the bar were more handsome. The whole vibe there was just luxurious. It was like Timmy said: "When the robes are softer than the girls' asses, the customer just knows he's living his best life."

Guy ordered a rye Manhattan. He counted in his head while the bartender worked, and it was his fifth drink of the day. Ever since his father had set this as the night, his nerves were shot. The only way he could keep his hands from shaking was to drink starting with breakfast.

Would his father pull the trigger or would he?

It was that question, asked in a dozen variations, that had

preoccupied Guy since the lunch meeting with his father. Even before, actually. In the days since, his ability to argue it either way truly impressed him and made him wonder if he should have tried out for the debate team in school. He could argue both sides, but he hated both answers — the one where he pulled the trigger and the one where he didn't.

Because, well, it had to happen sometime — so why not now? It was always the unspoken predicate when Guy joined the family business that no one in the La Rue family, or any Paris gang family, got through for very long without, in Passy's words, "getting wet." And while Guy didn't know if they laughed about it in later years — or bragged about it like men bragged about their first fucks — he'd never been privy to those kinds of conversations, and the people who worked for him were pretty much gang virgins, too. How they thought about it, he wasn't sure. But they all had done it. They all had pulled the trigger. And, well, why not now? Just get it over with.

But then, well, fuck. Clarice was never going to pull the trigger — of that, Guy was certain — and she was working in the family. And things were adapting, at least a little. The peace with the Levines seemed solid, and the money was rolling in, and the notion of gang wars seemed just a bit old, a bit 1930s. It seemed like a black-and-white movie more than anything, and maybe there would continue to be an evolution. Most of the violence came from the street money, but that was becoming a smaller and smaller part of the operation — and besides, that was broken bones, not bullets. Maybe Guy's would be the generation of the more corporate gang family, the one where money and payoffs solved virtually every problem.

And if that was at least possible, then why pull the trigger? Why not let his father? Then again, how might his father react to the whole thing? Henri would have thought it through, obviously. Would he see it as Guy's right as a young man in the business to do it? His right, or his obligation — because Serge Lemelin was his mess, after all? Or would he do what he could to shield his son, to delay the inevitable for as long as he could? And if he knew what his mother would think, and how against him pulling the trigger she would be, well, what were the odds that his father had clued her in to the problem? Pretty low, Guy concluded. Pretty fucking low.

So, around and around it had gone for days. It was spinning, still, when Lemelin emerged from the back area wearing a plush white robe. He looked at Guy's empty glass.

"Shit, did I take a long time?" he said.

"No, I was quick. Hadn't had any for days. Bang, bang, bang."

"You need to work on your multiplication tables."

"What the fuck are you talking about?"

"Multiplication tables," Lemelin said. "When you feel yourself getting close, starting thinking about the multiplication tables."

"That's bullshit."

"It's not bullshit, my friend. It'll slow you down. I got to three times nine tonight."

They both laughed, and ordered a drink, and talked about the wonders of Celeste. They talked about a bunch of things but not about the Pink Ballet. Then, after gulping another drink, Guy said, "I have a car waiting. We'll take you home — maybe after stopping off for one more. I know a new place."

The Stag was a crappy bar in the crappy part of the 9th. The La Rues had owned it for ages, and more than anything it provided a retirement job for one of their original soldiers. Tommy Quinn had fought with the Royal Warwickshire Regiment in the first war at Passchendaele and decided not to go home after the armistice. A French woman, apparently. He was a contemporary of Henri's father and Gérard but even older — pushing 80, probably. The clientele tended to be people his age in the early evening and underage kids a bit later on. When Guy and Serge Lemelin walked in, there was a combination — but Guy could see Lemelin's face fall after he looked around.

"No, not in here," Guy said. "The back room."

Lemelin perked up.

"More girls," Guy said.

"But we—"

"Not for screwing, just for looking at. Maybe touching. They do their interpretative dances, if you know what I mean."

"No fucking?"

"Well, maybe," Guy said.

But when they got to the back room — which was down a hallway and actually consisted of a garage that backed onto the alley behind the bar — there were no girls. There was only Henri — well, Henri and the half-empty bottle sitting on the cinder floor next to his chair. No glass.

He, too, had been thinking.

It was in 1934, late. December, just before Christmas. Henri was 21 at the time. There had never been a question about what he was going to do for a living. There had never even been a conversation. Big Jean's three sons — Little Jean, Henri, and Martin — were all destined to join the family business. Period. End of discussion. Actually, without discussion.

December, just before Christmas. The scam had been simple enough, the robbery of a delivery truck in the loading dock behind the big Galeries Lafayette on the Champs-Élysées. Fur stoles were the most valuable thing in the back, according to the guy they were paying in the Galeries Lafayette shipping department. There would be one driver, and one or two clerks from the store would come out after he rang the bell to help with the unloading. There would be no security, no trouble. The whole thing wouldn't take 10 minutes — a little shouting and waving of their guns, and then the furs would be out of the truck and into the back of their car.

It would be a cinch, except for the second guy accompanying the driver, the one with the shotgun.

The way they had arrayed themselves — perched behind parked vehicles — Henri was with his father on one side of where the delivery truck pulled in, and Little Jean and Martin were on the other side. Henri and Big Jean had the better view of the surprise emerging from the passenger side, the one carrying the shotgun and surveying the area. It was dark, though, because the La Rues had managed to put out the lights closest to the loading dock. The guy likely couldn't see anything.

But they saw him, Henri and Big Jean did.

And then Henri looked at his father.

And his father said nothing, just locked eyes.

Henri was 21. December, just before Christmas. In the years and decades that followed, he sometimes wondered if he had misread the signal. He knew he hadn't but he still couldn't help thinking that maybe his father was saying something else with that hard stare. But what?

Henri detached from his father's gaze. His hands were shaking, just a little, but he steadied his shotgun on the place in the back of the truck where you step up into the cargo area. It wasn't a tough shot but it wasn't a cinch either.

He stole a quick glance over his shoulder. His father was still staring, his face blank otherwise.

Henri turned again. The guard with the shotgun was scanning, scanning, and then he turned his back toward Henri.

Now or never, he thought.

Now.

And he blew the guy's head off.

And his father never said a word about it. The guard was dead, the driver and the two store clerks were defenseless and horrified besides, the furs were in the back of their car in about three minutes, and then they were off — Little Jean driving, Big Jean next to him, Henri and Martin in the back.

And his father never said anything. And that's what Henri was thinking about, the silence in that car that night and for all of the years afterward, when the door to the garage opened and Guy walked in with Serge Lemelin.

It took maybe three seconds for the whole thing to register in Lemelin's mind. He looked at Henri, then back at Guy, then back at Henri again. One second. Two seconds. Three seconds. Guy hit him in the back of the head with his pistol when the count got to four, and young Serge was asleep. He was not likely dreaming of Celeste, but of more pressing matters.

"Here, let me help you," Henri said, and the two of them, father and son, picked up Lemelin by the armpits and lifted him onto the chair where Henri had been sitting. Henri had a length of electrical cord stuffed into his coat pocket, and he bound Lemelin's wrists behind him, and then tied them to the chair. Guy watched, and his father said, "Wrists together first, then to the chair," and the son nodded.

When he was finished, Henri reached down to slap Lemelin awake. Guy could see what he was about to do and said, "Why? Better that he's knocked out, no?"

"We need to talk to him."

"Why?"

"To find out what he knows."

"Like I told you, I don't think he knows anything — he told me tonight they still haven't called him in for an interview."

"What he says when he's wearing one of Timmy's plush robes is likely different from what he'll say when he's tied to a chair and pissing himself," Henri said.

At which point, he slapped Lemelin awake. It took three slaps, and the third one was a real wallop.

"Once again," Henri said. It had been maybe five minutes since he started the questioning. It had begun gently, but the intensity was increasing. Another slap. A punch with a balled fist that knocked out a tooth and began the bleeding. His father had taken off his coat and his jacket along the way, and his shirt-sleeves were rolled up.

For his part, Serge Lemelin had, indeed, pissed himself. Piss, blood and tears. Didn't Churchill say something about that during the war?

Guy half laughed when the thought crossed his mind. Mostly, though, he fixated on the piss and the blood and the tears — and his hope that maybe there was something Lemelin could say that would change the outcome.

"Once again," Henri said, a second time, and Lemelin began blubbering the same facts: that he hadn't been questioned and that the La Rues had nothing to worry about.

Panicked, bawling, Lemelin looked at Henri and said, "I won't say anything. I promise."

Guy caught it immediately, as did his father.

"Won't?" Henri said.

Lemelin's eyes grew wide.

"When, Serge?" Henri said.

Lemelin's head fell.

"When, Serge?" Henri said. He was crouching right next to the chair, barely speaking above a whisper.

"Day after tomorrow, 10 a.m., prosecutor's office," Lemelin said. He never looked up, never saw Henri nod at Guy with their prearranged signal, never saw Guy club him again on the back of the head, knocking him out for the second time.

His father's pistol remained in the holster beneath his left armpit. He never showed it to Lemelin. The holster was enough.

Guy was holding his pistol by the barrel. It was how he had

clubbed Lemelin, but he continued to hold it that way. It seemed like less of a weapon somehow.

Ten, 15, maybe 20 seconds. Guy wouldn't make eye contact with his father, not until Henri said, "Here." From his coat pocket, he took a silencer that would screw into the barrel of Guy's pistol.

"How did you know?"

"Timmy told me," Henri said. It had been Timmy who supplied Guy with the pistol when he first took over the whorehouses. His advice had been simple: "Two hands and nothing fancy. Right in the heart."

Guy's hands were shaking, and he couldn't thread the silencer into the barrel. Without a word, without a hint of disdain, his father took the pistol and the silencer and screwed the two ends together. Then he handed the gun back to his son.

Nothing was being said, but everything was clear. The decision had been made, and maybe there had never been a choice. Lemelin was his mess, and it had to happen.

Guy stood behind Lemelin, who was still unconscious and slumped forward in the chair. Henri moved behind the chair, too. He stood next to Guy but not too close. He was about 10 feet away.

The pistol was a lot heavier because of the silencer. Guy lifted it, took a step forward, and rested it on the back of Lemelin's neck.

"No, a step back," Henri said, almost in a whisper.

Guy took a step back.

"Maybe in his mouth, to look like suicide?"

"Wouldn't wash — not with the bruises and the missing tooth," Henri said.

"So, won't the cops be all hepped up by the idea that it's a, well, an execution?" Guy said. He had a very hard time saying the word. Execution.

"I don't think so."

"Why not?"

"Because, for all they know, the cops themselves were the ones doing the executing," Henri said. "And if that's the case, they really don't want to know."

"But what about the people in the bar? They saw us."

"You've forgotten about Tommy Quinn," Henri said, motioning out toward the bar. "It's why I'm really not worried about the cops, either way — suicide, execution, whatever. Tommy's still on the payroll. Our friend here will be gone by morning, likely in pieces."

"That old man?" Guy said.

"Small pieces," Henri said.

Henri took another step back. Guy took that to mean that the time for conversation was over. His mind was racing so fast that it seemed like static from the radio. Time.

He lifted the pistol, and it really was heavier. He was having a lot of trouble holding it steady, but it would be okay. From maybe two feet away, he didn't think he could miss — and Serge Lemelin had not moved, not a muscle, since Guy had clubbed him with the pistol.

He stood there, shaking.

He took a deep breath.

And then, he heard his father say, barely above a whisper, "Two hands."

———

It was hours later, in a bar in the 17th that neither of them had ever been in. It was a boyfriend-girlfriend kind of place, and the tables were pretty full, but the bar itself was empty except for an old man sitting at the far end. The bartender could sense that they wanted to be alone and kept the chitchat to a minimum. For their part, Guy and Henri said nothing. They just drank, with Henri doing the pouring. They just drank and stared into the mirror behind the bar, looking at the couples talking and laughing and holding hands.

Hours and nearly a full bottle later, Guy finally said, "I don't know what I'm feeling."

"Numb for now, and the alcohol helps," Henri said. "It'll cost you some sleep for a while — completely normal. But it will pass — I can promise you that. It always does."

When it was closing time, Henri made a call, and one of Passy's boys arrived with a car. They drove Guy to his apartment, and Henri walked him to the door. They were both beyond shit-faced, stumbling up the steps, and they hugged after Guy managed to make the key work. In Guy's memory, it was always Henri who initiated the hug.

"You'll need new suits," Henri said.

"What for?"

"Jackets one size bigger than the pants," the father told the son, patting the shoulder holster he was wearing under his left armpit.

PART XIII

LOOSE ENDS

érard was sitting in Roger Cornette's office in the Mazarine Library. Jean Lemieux, who had never seen the place, was wandering around the reading room and gawping at its splendor. They had started talking and then stopped when one of Cornette's assistant librarians interrupted with a sheaf of documents that required signatures here, here, and here. Cornette signed them without reading.

"A Mazarine virgin? I can always tell the face," Cornette said. He gestured out toward Lemieux in the reading room and then he made like a fish getting ready to be hooked.

"Maybe a virgin virgin," Gérard said. "Don't know what he did before the seminary."

"Or after."

"Pretty sure about after."

"Gérard , my old friend. So naive sometimes. I mean, I'm the librarian, the one with his head in the books all day, and you, well..."

"I see people for who they are."

"Not who you want them to be?"

"Who they are," Gérard said. "I know who I am, and I know who you are, and I know who Father Jean Lemieux is."

"And who's that?"

"A friend. A spiritual counselor. A counselor of all sorts."

Cornette arched an eyebrow. Gérard caught the skepticism instantly. Before he could say something, there was another light knock on the open door jamb. A woman this time.

"Just a reminder — 12:30 at Maxim's, yes?" she said.

"Yes, yes."

"Important to be on time."

"They're all important," Cornette said. Then, as the woman withdrew, he turned back to Gérard and said, "Madame Beliveau. Lunch."

"Of Beliveau and Beliveau?"

"The widow, yes."

"The rich widow?"

"Yes, the rich widow and library benefactor."

The way Gérard's chair was turned, he could see Father Lemieux taking another gawping lap around the reading room. The place was quiet, only two patrons, one of whom was examining what appeared to be an ancient ledger with a magnifying glass.

"You have help here, no?" Gérard said.

"Obviously — you've seen. Of course I have help. I'm the boss, and I don't do shit — other than have lunch with patrons and argue with you about books."

"The Spaniards next," Gérard said.

"Maybe."

"But, you know, could you still handle all of the paperwork around here, the orders and payroll and whatever else, without help?"

"Probably. Maybe."

"Exactly," Gérard said. "Maybe. Or, maybe not. And I make decisions that go a bit beyond purchasing orders and publishing companies. So, Father Lemieux is my help."

Cornette thought for a second, taking it all in. The two of them, friends since school, were past 70. He understood.

"Except, I mean, he's not family. And haven't you always said..."

"I trust him," Gérard said.

"And Henri and the rest?"

"I trust him," Gérard said.

"And will he sit in on your meeting with your friend?"

"No, no. But we will ride back together in the car, and I will brief him before any of it slips my mind."

"Is that happening?"

"Just a little. Nothing serious yet, but just a little. Small slips. And you?"

"I can't remember what I had for lunch," Cornette said. "But I can picture like it was yesterday the time that you and me and Willy stole that case of wine from the back of Old Garreau's shop."

"What were we?"

"Fifteen. I remember where we drank it."

"The cemetery," Gérard said.

"Montmartre Cemetery. I remember the name of the grave we pissed on."

Gérard shrugged.

"Mondieu," Cornette said. "And we threw up on the one next to it. Carbon. You could even see how red it was in the dark, the puke."

They talked for a few more minutes until Old Joe Levine arrived. Cornette countered the Spaniards with "something lighter, more fun. Maybe American Westerns. Have you ever heard of Zane Grey?"

"Seems a bit unserious, no?" Gérard said.

"Not everything in life needs to be serious," Cornette said.

The café at the five-point intersection, pretty close to the catacombs, was where Henri and David Levine met.

"The 14th, it's really fine," Henri said. He half waved at the traffic whizzing by and the apartments that surrounded the square, five- or six-story apartments with shops at street level, five- or six-story apartments that would not have looked out of place in almost any Paris neighborhood. Maybe not near the top of the butte in Montmartre, or in the older parts of the 2nd and 3rd where Levine lived, but almost anywhere.

"No better than fine," Levine said.

They sat outside, under the awning. The weather had warmed a bit, and the sun was out. They both eyed the menu and settled on omelettes.

"Can't fuck up an omelette," Henri said.

"In the 14th, or anywhere near where Sleepy JoJo is within reach, they can fuck up anything."

The eggs were fine, as it turned out. Henri's car was double-parked along the curb on Avenue Jean Moulin, and David's was just behind it. Their drivers were chatting when they weren't dropping the names La Rue and Levine to passing cops who wanted them to move on. Henri watched one such encounter, and saw the cop walk quickly away, and he smiled. The name La Rue meant something, even over on this side of the river. Unless it was the name Levine, of course, although Henri never really pondered that possibility.

David looked at his watch.

"Ten minutes, give or take," he said.

Henri looked at his.

"I have 11 minutes."

They both resumed eating. Neither man was comfortable with the arrangement, but it was what it was. Philip Tanguay's stunt in the casino had cost the Levines a life and a little bit of money. The shit he pulled with the mail train cost both the Levines and the La Rues a lot of money, with both stations now in the "frozen zone." The "lot of money" had forced the alliance on this matter — much more than the dead Levine soldier at the casino. That was just the reality of their world. Henri got it, and so did David, but neither felt good about it.

Old Joe and Gérard had worked out the arrangement and then delivered the edict, Old Joe to his son and Gérard to his nephew. Because the Levines, as it turned out, had the better police connections in the 14th, they did the initial surveillance

— and as it turned out, Philip Tanguay was such an amateurish idiot that they began tailing him within two hours of starting their search. As it turned out, the kid spent time in a student bar, the Descartes' Horse, every afternoon-into-evening, and then slept alone in the same flat on Rue de Rungis.

With that, Passy and Harry Bontemps — David's right hand — took the information about Tanguay's habits, along with a detailed map of the 14th, and decided on the place. Freddy and Marc Savitz, the best guns in the two families, were tasked with carrying out the plan.

"Four minutes, or five," David Levine said.

"Five," Henri said.

They both went back to their eggs, which had cooled quickly. Henri took a final bite and left the congealed final third of the omelette on the plate. At the same time, David was wiping his plate with a piece of toast.

Two minutes.

Or, three.

"It's a good plan," Henri said.

"I trust Harry more than my wife," David said.

"Passy, too."

The waiter brought two fresh coffees. Philip Tanguay, besides sleeping in the same place and drinking in the same place, also ate lunch in the same place every day — or, at least, on the four consecutive days that the Levines had eyes on him. The Redbird was a typical hole-in-the-wall kind of place, not as nice as the café where Henri and David were eating but not a dump, either. It was on a quieter street, too. From where they would be parked, Freddy and Marc would see Tanguay for almost a block as he walked from his apartment to The Redbird. After some debate, Marc was given the passenger seat along the curb — the Levines had lost a man at the casino, after all. Freddy would drive and be prepared to finish what Marc started, if necessary, from his spot pretending to inspect a problem with the left front tire.

One minute.

Or, two.

"This is, uh…"

"Unusual," David Levine said.

"Yes, that. But I have to ask, you don't see it as…"

"Customary?"

"The start of something, right, customary?" Henri said.

Levine took a sip of coffee.

"In this case, our interests are aligned," he said.

Now, Henri sipped.

"I agree," he said. "And that, I think, should be our touchstone. Our guide. I have no interest in running every La Rue family move past you. I can't."

"You can't, I can't," David said.

"Except in the 10th, where we share the train stations and have—"

"An understanding."

"Yes, an understanding. The problem is, well, the old men."

David Levine nodded.

"They are closer than we imagined — at least, closer than I imagined," Henri said.

David nodded again.

"It's the beauty of old men, though," David said. "They are old men and then they are dead men."

With that, David Levine raised his hand and snapped his fingers. Dead. Like that.

Time.

Or, one minute.

Philip Tanguay's arrival at The Redbird had barely varied: 12:12, 12:13, 12:14, 12:14. Freddy and Marc were in place at noon straight up, just in case. They figured on 12:13 as the time — that was what the plan said. Marc spotted Philip Tanguay first, about a block from the café. It was 12:11.

"Right on time," he said.

Freddy got out of the car and kneeled down next to the driver's side front tire and pretended to examine it. He had a sawed-off shotgun in his coat pocket — an overcoat with an especially deep pocket. Marc, sitting in the car, had the same. Freddy wondered if they had the same tailor.

Tanguay crossed the intersection and was about a hundred feet from the front door of The Redbird. Marc Savitz had the clearer shot, but Freddy had a more than acceptable angle himself.

A hundred feet became 50, and 50 became 25. Freddy looked over at Marc. The shotgun was still in his lap.

Freddy looked again. Twenty-five feet. Twenty. The street was quiet. There were no civilians in the way. He looked over at Marc again. Still, the shotgun was in his lap.

Fuck it, Freddy thought.

He only needed the one shot. He was pretty sure that he got Philip Tanguay in the eye. The right eye.

When Freddy got back into the car and sped off, Marc Savitz began screaming. If someone had been in the backseat making a transcript of the two of them ranting and yelling over each other, Savitz's most-used phrase would have been "La Rue motherfucker." Freddy's would have been "fucking Jewish pussy."

About three minutes later, the car sped by Henri La Rue and David Levine. They were still at the café, still under the awning. The check had been split, and they were finishing their coffee between peeks at their wristwatches.

The speeding car honked three times when it reached the café at the five-point intersection — one long blast on the horn followed by two shorter ones.

Henri and David shook hands and headed for their separate cars. It was done.

PART XIV

NEW REALITIES

"Talk to Guy?" Sylvie said. She and Henri were walking the 200-odd steps from their apartment to Gérard's.

"The other day, yeah."

"How did he sound to you?"

"Fine."

"I talked to him today for about two minutes. He sounds, I don't know, just off. Tired or something."

"He is working his ass off," Henri said. "And he's doing well. I mean, very well."

They turned the corner and Sacré Coeur came into view. Sylvie had been pretty much morose since the business with Lucien Richard on the front page of *France-Soir*. It had been more than a week, and Henri was almost certain she had not seen Richard. In the end, even if the charges didn't stick, the picture in the newspaper had been enough. The fling was over, and the sadness had filled the apartment like a cloud — until that day, right after lunch.

The invitation had arrived only that afternoon — by phone from Father Lemieux — and she hadn't been able to close her mouth ever since.

As they walked over, making the left when the street dead-ended into Sacré Coeur, she repeated herself for about the fifth time when she turned to Henri and said, "You know that I've never eaten a meal in that house."

"So I've heard," Henri said.

"I mean, never."

"There were nibbles at the Christmas drinks."

"Nibbles aren't a fucking meal," Sylvie said.

"They can be."

"You know what I'm saying."

"Yes, dear, I do," Henri said.

He did know what she was saying. Gérard did coffee for

daytime meetings and drinks at night. He did not do dinner — well, almost never. If Sylvie had never eaten a meal there, Henri could count his times on one hand.

It was a table set for eight — Henri and Sylvie, Martin and Marie, Michel and Romy, and Gérard and Father Lemieux. Silent Moe was not included, the kids weren't included, no one was included but those eight. And, as Sylvie said, "Seven would have made more sense, don't you fucking think?"

"Yes, I fucking think," Henri said.

They let that lie there as they made their way through the consommé and the salad. If Martin and Michel were thinking the same thing, Henri couldn't be sure. He had Sylvie on one side and Romy on the other, and the table wasn't very big, and if he could get away with a snide whisper to his wife, well, that was it as far as intrigue was concerned.

Next, the servers brought out a massive chateaubriand, with potatoes and asparagus on the side. Servers. Henri had never seen servers in Gérard's house. The cook, yes — but she worked only half-days, lunch and dinner, and only Monday to Friday. Servers, never.

They all ooh-ed and aah-ed at the the arrival of the massive piece of beef. Before taking a second slice, Sylvie leaned over and said, "I mean, it's actually good. The cheap old bastard. I mean, really good."

When it was time for coffee, cognac, cheese, and fruit, Gérard cleared his throat and said, "Ladies, if you could indulge an old man and take yours in the sitting room, we have a bit of business to discuss. If you could indulge me."

"Uh-oh," Sylvie said.

The three women got up, and Sylvie looked across at Father Lemieux. The priest was remaining nailed to his chair, pouring a measure of the cognac for himself and for Gérard. She saw it, and she saw that Henri saw it. Their eyes locked in the kind of glance that every old married couple knew. It was communicating without words, and it was communicating with a point.

Or, as husband and wife said to themselves, "Fuuuuck."

During the dinner, Gérard had raised his glass and said, "I am toasting myself. To my good health. To Lourdes. To faith. To my spiritual strength, which has led to my physical strength. And to the man who has nourished all of that."

Gérard looked at Lemieux at that point and clinked his glass first. And, well, fine. It had been hard to figure out what had been ailing Gérard without a medical diagnosis, but there was no denying his improvement or that you could date it to the trip to Lourdes. And, well, fine. Mind over body, or some such shit. But it was long past that toast, after the meal, and while the women had departed the priest was nailed to the chair. And Gérard was clearing his throat again.

He began talking about Clarice's success in that quarter, about how she had pledged a 50 percent return on their money and produced a 62 percent return instead. He looked at Henri and said, "I know you all had unspoken reservations, and you, Henri, most of all. But 62 percent is 62 percent. No one could argue with the decision, I don't believe."

Gérard continued to look at Henri, and Henri nodded. If the old man only knew how he had assisted Clarice, well... It was better kept as a secret, at least for now.

The old man went on to talk about "the recent cooperation with the Levine family." "Recent cooperation" as a euphemism for "murder" was an interesting rhetorical maneuver, but, whatever. Henri was waiting for the predicate, worried about the predicate — that Gérard saw even more cooperation with the Levines in the future. But he never said it out loud, and Henri considered that a victory.

Gérard took another sip, and then he looked over to the priest sitting to his right. He said, "No interruptions here," and then he took another sip.

Fuuuuck.

"As you all know, Jean here has been assisting me with my ledgers for a little while now," Gérard said. "He has straightened out books that had become a mess since Izzy died. And as he has done that, we have become closer."

Closer, Henri thought. Christ, had Guy been right?

"I have come to value his counsel," Gérard said.

Henri looked at Martin and Michel. Both were transfixed on the old man.

"I have come to see the wisdom of his perspective," Gérard said. "He is from outside the family, true enough, but my trust in Jean is implicit. It is complete. And being from outside he offers a slant on things that I could not possibly come up with on my own. Even with my eyes, which have seen so much, well, the lenses have always been from the inside looking out. Jean offers a different point of view. I find it to be a valuable point of view. Quite valuable."

Henri looked at Lemieux. The priest was looking down at his drink, at his hands.

"Gérard," Henri said.

"No interruptions, please."

Henri wanted to say out loud what Marin and Michel must have been thinking, what Sylvie would have been screaming if she had heard. That is, that a goddamned priest — a briefcase priest at that — could have no possible value to add to an operation that employed whores, and leg-breakers, and men adept in the use of firearms. No value. None. But he kept quiet. No interruptions, please.

"It is my intention, with your approval, to formalize the La Rue family's relationship with Father Jean Lemieux," Gérard said. "He will be living in this house six or seven nights a week. He will be available to be my counselor at all times, other than a few hours a week when he must continue to advise the cardinal on the finances of the archdiocese. His focus will be on the La Rue family. His primary focus. His overwhelming focus. To advise me, and listen to me, and counsel me in my decisions as head of the family."

Henri looked at Martin and Michel again. Still transfixed.

"I propose that, just as I receive two percent of everything, Father Lemieux will also receive two percent. That will be in recognition of his value to the family. In addition, he will receive a share of the quarterly profit sharing. Instead of the four of us each getting 25 percent from the pot, we now will receive 22 percent and Father Lemieux will receive 12 percent."

Jesus Christ.

Martin and Michel, still transfixed — although he did see Michel take the quickest of peeks in Martin's direction.

"Gérard, I must—" Henri said.

"No interruptions, please."

That had been Gérard's strategy all along. This had to be a surprise if it was to work, he figured. There could not be any discussion. He had to hit them between the eyes with it — Henri especially — and then he had to hope. He could pull rank in the end and just order it, but he was trying this way. Henri was his own case, but Martin the idiot owed him for years of protection, and Michel owed him for his very existence.

"I don't think we need a discussion," Gérard said. "Better to go with our gut here, all of us. So, just a vote. This isn't a democracy, but just a vote. Agree or not?"

"Hell no," Henri said. Then, he folded his arms and sat back in his chair. The way he figured it, Martin would follow. Christ, he had protected his sorry ass since they were kids. As for Michel, he was just a greedy asshole, and this was real money

Gérard was talking about. The way Henri reckoned it — and it was reckoning by instinct because there really hadn't been time to do a proper calculation — he got his "no" out first, when it would mean the most.

All eyes turned to Martin, next in line by age and by tradition. When his younger brother never looked in his direction, not for a second, Henri sensed something. Something not good.

"Yes," Martin said.

Gérard grinned. It wasn't a democracy, but with this vote, he would do no worse than 2-2. And even Henri would acknowledge that a tie went to the boss/uncle.

But, maybe not. Henri stared hard at Michel. A second no vote would give him a chance to argue. Gérard couldn't shut down the conversation forever. And if he could argue, he could make his dumbass brother see.

They all stared at Michel. And then, for the second time, Henri saw him take the quickest of looks at Martin. Martin did not reply with any kind of gesture. His face was impassive.

Michel cleared his throat.

"Yes," he croaked.

Jesus Christ. How could that thieving motherfucker? Henri was dumbfounded, but that was that. There really could be no argument after a 3-1 vote. He had no idea what happened after that, after he said, "Excuse me," and got up from the table. It was after a silent walk back to their apartment that Henri told Sylvie all of it. She was dumbfounded, too.

"Martin," she said.

"Is a goddamned idiot."

"You're missing the point."

"Meaning?"

"Meaning that regardless of the magic beans your uncle ate at Lourdes, he isn't going to be around forever," Sylvie said. "And when he isn't, well, now that briefcase priest is going to be a complication. And now your idiot brother... I don't know."

"I thought he would follow me," Henri said, half to himself.

"That's the point you've been missing. That he was independent enough to go the other way. And that... that chiseling Michel followed him."

They sat and drank. Henri had a hundred thoughts, and attempted to voice one of them, but then he stopped himself. Sylvie started once and stopped, too.

Then, finally, she said, "We've always thought the one thing. I mean, ever since Big Jean and Little Jean died."

"You mean, after Gérard..."

Sylvie nodded.

"My grandfather to my father," Henri said. "My father to his brother Gérard. Gérard to me, the oldest nephew. All clean lines. All logical."

Henri poured them each another measure. The bottle was empty.

And Sylvie said, "Clean lines. And, well, after tonight, I'm not sure it's all going to be so simple and guaranteed anymore."

I hope you enjoyed *Power*, the second book in my La Rue family crime thriller series. The third book in the series, *Rivals*, can be ordered here:

My Book

In addition, I'd love for you to sign up for my newsletter so that you can receive updates about future books in the La Rue family crime thriller series. If you sign up, you will receive a free novella that is a prequel to my first series. It features Alex Kovacs, an everyman who tries to do the right thing as the Nazis are preparing to invade his home in Austria in 1938 and ends up as a spy, and then in the French Resistance, and then as a spy again during the Cold War.

The title of the prequel that you will receive for free is *Ominous Austria.* To get it, just click here:

https://dl.bookfunnel.com/ur7seb8qeg

Printed in Great Britain
by Amazon

45852750R00128